Be a Girl

- An LGBTQ+, First Time, Voluntary Feminization, Short-Read Romance

by Barbara Deloto and Thomas Newgen

To purchase another copy of this book, or to see our other books go to
https://www.amazon.com/Barbara-Deloto/e/B00J21HWA4/

A few of our other books
Realizing Jessica - A Femboy Gets Fem and Discovers Inner Passions and Love
Desires- Fantasy Becomes Reality for an Occasional Crossdresser
Trannies - Two Guys Get Fem
Jessica's Turn: A Gender-Bending LGBT Romance
Frat House - A Gender-Bending LGBT Romance
Finishing School - A Boy Is Sent to a Girls' Finishing School - An LGBT Romance
All Dolled Up: A Student Gets Fem - An LGBT Romance
Sissy Boyfriend
Being Candy
Paying My Dues
Virtual Vacation
Filling in For Her
His New Dress
Her Gift to Him
Telling Her
Feminized to Win
Crossdreaming
Feminized by Her
Taking it for the Team
Feminized Men: A Guide for Increased Joy in Crossdressing
Feminized Vacation
The House of Enchanted Feminization
Heirs to Heiresses
Connected
Our Gift to Each Other
Girlfriend
Insatiable
A New Taste for Life
Spellbound
Femboy Guild

1

Classes had ended, and I wasn't going home for Christmas. I could have, but I'd have to either change the way I act and dress and present myself and fake being macho, or face the wrath of my old man. I told them I had to work on a project over break and let it go over that. They knew engineering took a lot of time, so the excuse worked.

Woo hoo! This would be the best Christmas ever. I already had plans for the evening with my buddy Cassie, so I cleaned up my desk and put my books aside for a well-needed break. I did laundry, vacuumed and dusted my one-bedroom apartment, and brought it back to respectability after the weeks of neglect.

When it was all done, I took a long bath and shaved my whole body. I hated body hair and the way it held sweat and made me seem like some wild animal. After I dried and fluffed my curly blonde hair and put it in a ponytail, I put in my new fake-diamond stud earrings, two in each earlobe. A little eyeliner and mascara made my eyes pop and some lip gloss would protect my lips from the cold weather. I used some clear nail polish to protect my decently long fingernails. Long enough to be shaped nicely.

I slid into some stretchy, black-satin sheath underwear and a pair of knee-high socks and topped them with a pair of size 4 women's, stretch, boot-cut jeans (they fit better than men's), and a three inch heeled brown leather boot. At five foot five, I could use the extra height and so what if they were women's boots? They were pretty plain anyway.

I put on a black button-down collar shirt and tucked it in. Inspecting myself in the mirror, I slid the belt through the loops. I smiled at myself seeing the really cute, and highly intelligent guy that I was, confident some girl would soon fall in love with me though none had so far. I sprayed cologne on, loaded my pockets and left.

Cassie was already waiting for me at the bar. He beamed as I walked in and waved. His reddish-brown, wavy hair glistened from the light above him. I sat on the stool next to him and we gently shook hands and patted each other's shoulders. "Happy vacation, Riley!" he said as he slid a frothy beer to me and held his up for a bump.

"Happy vacation, buddy. Thanks for stickin' around for the break with me." I took a long swig of the beer.

"No problem. This'll be way more fun. So, we have a lot to look forward to. All the frats are having Christmas parties and they're all on different nights. We have plenty to do, chasing chicks at them all."

"You bet." I caught the attention of the bartender. "You hungry, Cassie? I'm famished."

"Yeah. I'm ready for a pizza."

The bartender came over and leaned on the bar. "Ready?"

I nodded. "Anchovies, sausage, and pineapple, deep dish please."

He shook his head, mumbled something about the anchovies and pineapple, wrote it down, and left.

Cassie laughed. "No one likes our combinations on pizza."

"Ha! I know. Fuck those mundane assholes. The salt and sweet go great." I sipped the beer. "SO, you think we have a chance at some babes?"

"Well, they all have to dress up for the parties, so at least we'll see some stockings and heels and party dresses."

"We could see that at the mall."

"You know what I mean. Girls in those clothes."

"Right. And what's gonna make them treat us any different than they always do? What can we do differently?"

He put his elbow on the bar and rested his head on his hand. "Hmm. Good point." He lifted his head and looked around the bar.

"One thing girls do at those parties is they group together. You know. They're safer or more confident somehow when there are more of them. We approach the group like we do and the first one that casts a bad glance or unfavorable body language at us ends up turning them all off to us instantly and we're finished. We need to get past that point."

"Right. We have to be accepted, not rejected."

"You know that once they learn how smart we are and what nice guys we are, we'd have a chance if we could get that far. Unfortunately, they go for the hunks. The look at the cover, not what's inside."

I slapped his thigh. "Exactly! How do we get past that? Sounds like another problem waiting for an engineer to solve it, right? We can figure it out."

He nodded and sipped his beer.

I sipped my beer and looked around the bar. Three girls were chatting at the other end. I watched as a fourth girl came in looking lost and scanned the place. She made her way to the girls at the end, and they introduced themselves to her and all shook limp hands. One of them ordered a drink for her.

I poked Cassie in the side. "See That?" I motioned with my head.

"Yeah? A girl arrived and joined the other three."

"Right. The one that came in was alone, and they didn't know her. They introduced themselves and bought her a drink. Guys don't do that for guys. We just need to be part of the girl club."

Cassie looked at me, dumbfounded. "Riley, am I hearing you say what you're saying?" He put his index finger across his lips, thumb under it. His clear painted nails glinted in the light. His eyeliner'd and mascara dusted eyelashes fluttered nervously.

I shrugged. "Why not? I think it might be fun. Heck, we're both already wearing eyeliner, mascara, lip gloss, and clear nail polish. All we'd be doing is stepping it up a little and going to the mall and after we could walk into those parties and have a free pass straight into the gangs of girls." I looked over at the four girls at the end of the bar. They were all getting to know the new girl, touching each other playfully. They even kissed her cheek. "See that, Cassie?"

"I did. I think you're right. It might be our best bet. But when do we let them know we're guys?"

"Heck, I don't know. At least we can start a conversation."

"True. Okay. I'm game." He looked me up and down. He ran his hand through my hair. "Nice hair. I think we should get our hair styled, though. May as well do it right." He lifted my hand and looked at my nails. "Your nails are perfect. A little gel and they'd be gorgeous. Mine need fake nails put on."

"Uh... haircut? Nails?"

"Riley! You want to look right or not? We have to do it up well. Can't have them guessing we're guys until it's time to tell them."

"True. Okay. I'm in all the way."

Our pizza arrived.

2

We scoffed that pizza down and were off to the mall. We had a few hours, so we made use of it so we could go to the first party tomorrow night.

We had our hair done, and it was amazing the way it changed our looks. The styling and highlighting made it really feminine and pretty. The girls doing us had a ball, too. I had my nails gelled and Cassie had fake ones put on.

From there, we walked to a women's lingerie and undergarment shop and the girl our age had a ball helping us find bras, panties, stockings, and pantyhose, and she fitted us with gel breast forms, giving us cleavage. We wore the bras and gel breast forms out of the store and continued our trek.

We tried on different dresses and critiqued each other, realizing if we had hard-ons, like we did trying them on, we'd have to have dresses that wouldn't show them and we ended up finding the hottest, shortest, most cleavage producing mini dresses with layered, flared, or bubble hems that made it to right below the top of the thighs. Riley chose a hunter green satin bubble hem, and I chose a maroon bubble hem. We looked totally festive and put together side by side. Shoes were next, and we found strappy stilettos in silver with matching purses and silver wraps to put over our shoulders and tie below our cleavage.

Our party outfits were done. We sat on a couch in the center of the mall reviewing our buys and making sure we had everything. I shook my head. "Shit, that was expensive."

Cassie shrugged. "It'll be worth it. Think of it as an investment." He dug through a bag. "Shit. We didn't get any perfume. We need perfume."

"Right. We'll stop on the way out and get some."

"Rings, necklaces, earrings, bracelets."

"Crap. Yup. There's a cheap jewelry store on the way out, too." I stopped going through our things and looked around the mall. I took a deep breath, watching girls go by. "You know. We'll need some warm coats. And...now that our hair and nails are done. We need some casual girls' clothes until we flip our presentation back to guys."

"Okay. Tomorrow we do the Goodwill and Salvation Army stores and we can stock up cheaply."

"Good idea. Man, I'm beat."

"Me too." Cassie's eyes flitted over my face, chest, and hair. "You make a pretty girl, Riley. Your voice fits too. No one will know."

"Thanks, I get hot looking at myself. It makes me think I'm a little fucked up. I guess we need to use different pronouns now, too." I looked Cassie over. "You're pretty fucking hot, too. I mean. No one would guess." I throbbed in my sheath underwear. "Uh… I mean, you'd be a perfect girlfriend for me… if we were like that."

Cassie nodded. "Likewise, *girl*." I swear I saw her eyes tear up a little. She blinked quickly and looked away. She checked her watch. "Well, *girl*. What say we pick up the jewelry and perfume, take our cache home and put it away? What time you wanna start tomorrow?" She rested her long nailed hand on my jeans and gazed into my eyes with a little smile. It unsettled me. She was so inviting, and we already knew each other so well, but she was a he, right? It flustered me.

"Uh...as early as we can. When do Goodwill and Salvation army open? I want to be stabilized and done with this project, so I don't have to think about it anymore."

"They open at nine."

"Okay. Right now I wanna stop and get a cheap denim mini, a V-neck sweater, a cheap casual purse and a cheap pair of high wedge heel boots for shopping in tomorrow. There's a cheap juniors shop on the way out that we looked in for the dresses and they had those on sale. I should have bought them then."

We stood, wrapped our arms in our bags, and trekked through the mall to finish our shopping.

3

In the morning, I was so excited I couldn't lie in bed any longer and got up at 6:30AM. I showered and shaved the little nubble I had anywhere and promptly did my hair, eyeliner, and mascara. It made me realize we didn't buy any other makeup like blush, contouring, or real lipstick. We'd have to stop for that. Man! It was a bitch being a girl all the way.

The anticipation was killing me and I couldn't wait to slide into my sheer brown pantyhose and then figured out I'd have to cut out the crotch a bit or be destined to lowering them every time I peed. Scissors fixed that and I put them back on. I slid on a pair of stretchy, silky panties, my bra and gel breast forms, and adjusted my cleavage. I slid up the denim miniskirt, zipped it, and put on the pink V-neck sweater. Next, my new brown faux-suede four-inch wedge-heeled boots slid on easily and I zipped them up to hug my calves.

I loaded my plain brown leather purse, sprayed perfume on and put that in the purse, then grabbed a puffy short winter coat that could pass for a girl's or a guy's and put it on. Checking myself in the mirror, I was perfect! Best I ever looked, actually. I grinned while I turned back and forth, admiring myself and throbbing in my panties from how sexy I looked.

I took my coat off, made some breakfast, and texted Cassie.

She responded immediately. "I couldn't sleep anymore either. I'm ready to go if you are. Want me to pick you up, *girl*?"

I texted back. "Perfect. I'll be done by the time you get here and I'll be waiting outside." Cassie was now a *girl* friend not a *guy* friend, and I was her *girl*friend. Oh well, who cares, so what? Why not? I was never more in my skin and was having a ball.

I cleaned up the kitchen, grabbed my coat and purse, and walked out. The sun was blinding off the snow covered ground.

People moved about on the busy street. I leaned back against the building to get out of the wind. The shocking chill whipped under my skirt and across my thighs in a way I never experienced before. I realized I was very vulnerable in this outfit and it made me throb in my panties, understanding I was in a very standard outfit for women—a vulnerable, not runnable heel, wearing a short skirt that the wind or anything else could get right under. Perhaps that's why women dressed like this, for the sexy ambiance it brought. It could be that's why I felt sexier than I ever had.

Cassie pulled up by the sidewalk and leaned over the passenger seat, waving at me. I heard the door unlock, and I opened it and climbed in. "Morning Cassie. Brrr. It's cold when that wind blows under your skirt!" I laughed.

She laughed and nodded her pretty new hairdo, waiting to pull out. "Sure is. You should try cleaning snow off the car this way and sitting your hardly covered panties on a cold leather seat. You know, we forgot lipstick and shit. Dressed in fancy dresses like we bought, we need to get blush and contouring and all that stuff."

"Yup. This morning, I realized that." I looked over at Cassie as she drove. Her face showed her happiness. The sun glistened off her nails and highlighted hair. "You look like an angel in the sunshine, sweetie. If you don't mind me calling you sweetie."

"Heck no. Girls do that right? We have to be in the role... *honey*. Thanks for the compliments. You're really pretty, too." She reached her hand over and patted my stockinged thigh. "Very sexy too."

My hand touched her sheer, silky, suntan colored stockinged thigh. "I even feel sexy too…and you even feel sexy to me too." My hand couldn't resist gliding along her sexy leg. "Is my touch here nice to you? Is this okay? Your pantyhose are so nice to touch. I love my hand on them."

She nodded nervously.

"I have to see how it is when someone touches *my* legs in pantyhose." I took her hand off the console and slid it on my thigh. "Mmm, it's very sensual. You can keep doing that all day."

Surging uncontrollably in my panties, I recrossed my legs, and she removed her hand and I took mine away. My heart raced. Her face was full of fear. "Forgive me, Cassie. I shouldn't have done that. I got carried away. My mistake. Please forgive me?"

She nodded nervously. "Uh...yeah...no...no big deal...*sister*. Girls do those things right? I just have to remember we need to act like girls if we're gonna fit in.... right? We *should* touch each other more, like girls do. Shouldn't we?"

"Of course. Why didn't I think of that? Then what I did was okay. Right?"

"Yeah, right? We *should* do those things." She nodded and pulled into the drugstore. "Right. We *should*. Okay, cosmetics."

We stepped in and browsed the makeup and all the tools and lipsticks and found ones that seemed to be nice enough and not too expensive. We left and drove to the Goodwill store.

No one was the wiser about our charade. Women seemed to treat us better than before when we were just femboys. At least now we weren't halfway girls to them, I guess. I was really enjoying being the new me.

"Cassie, what do you think of this coat? Is it over the top?" I slid my arms into the plush, silky, rabbit fur coat that was just long enough to cover my party dress.

Cassie ran her hand over it and looked me up and down, having me turn around. "I love it! If you're not getting it, I sure am. Let me try it on!"

Her face lit up when she wrapped the high collar around her chin. I squeezed her shoulders and ran my hands down her arms to hold her hands and take her in. I couldn't resist giving her a peck on the lips. "You take it. You're so gorgeous in it."

Her eyes were wide.

"Sorry. Girls kiss girls, right?"

She looked around. "Sorry. Right." She laughed a nervous laugh. "Thanks so much. I adore it. Maybe we'll find another coat for you. Twenty bucks is incredible for it."

We shopped and filled a cart with five-dollar purses, six-dollar shoes, heels and boots, skirts, dresses, party dresses for twelve dollars. It was crazy the things we found. Some things were brand new and still with tags on.

We finished that store off and drove to Salvation army and low and behold, there was another rabbit fur coat for me. It was the same length, but instead of a cream color, it was more of a tan. I was in heaven.

By the time we were done, we both had more clothes than we ever owned as guys. The trunk was stuffed like a turkey on thanksgiving. "My god, Cassie! Where will we put it all?"

"We'll make room. I think we both like our new selves well enough to be doing this for a while. I already know I'm donating my boy clothes to Goodwill. Girls' clothes are way more fun than guys. Let's get these things washed and put away. We can do the laundry at my house and you can help bag up my boy clothes and then we can put away my things and go to your place and do yours. Then we'll spilt up and get ready for the party and I'll pick you up. Sound good?" Her eyes were bright and her face glowing with joy.

We stood by the trunk of the car; the wind blowing snow under my skirt and around my legs. She stared at me as I did at her. Moving closer, I grasped her arm and looked deep into her eyes, then glanced around and stole a kiss from her. Staring at her, I waited. Her eyes seemed to get watery, then quickly she looked around and snatched a kiss off my lips and laughed. "Stop it, sister. This is gettin' to be too much fun." She nudged me toward my side of the car. "We have lots to do. Let's go."

4

It was weird packing away our guy clothes. We were both pretty quiet when we did it, and it was as if we just wanted to get it over with. Neither of us had any remorse and the weird feelings left when we could put away our new, more exciting, more fitting clothes. Who would think clothes could make a person so different?

We finished our work at Cassie's and were just about done at my place. Cassie was stuffing another trash bag with my old things. "I'll help you drag your old clothes down to my car and then I'll leave from there. I can't wait to get dressed for the party." She stuffed my old sneakers into the big black trash bag and cinched the top shut.

She stood and smiled at me. "Thanks for your help, Riley. This was interesting so far."

My eyes flitted across her face. Her eyes met mine and glanced away out the window. "It was."

She looked at her watch. "Okay. Gotta go. See you soon."

She turned to leave, and I stopped her with my hand on her shoulder. I turned her to face me. I kissed her quickly on the lips and gave her a hug; our gel breast forms crushing into each other delightfully. "Mmm, this is so nice. Thanks. Can't wait to see you in your party dress. We'll be in like flint with some hot babes tonight, right?"

Flustered, she straightened her clothes and ran a long nailed hand through her hair. "You bet, Riley." She left.

I took out my party clothes and things and placed them on the bed. Stripping, I stepped into the shower, rinsed off, then did my hair and makeup with my new products. Contour, blush, eye-shadow, mascara, 24 hour lipstick all applied... all the while I was growing more aroused by my face looking back at me. I was my own sex kitten.

Seated on the bed, I deliciously glided the gossamer thin, sheer suntan pantyhose on with the crotch cut out, then slid up a fresh pair of silky, stretchy pink panties and tucked my hard cock against my tummy. Guiding the matching bra around me and fastening the hooks, I slid the hooks around to the back and loaded my gel breast forms into it, making lovely cleavage and more throbbing in my panties.

I slid the silky satin lining of the dress over my legs, sending a shiver through me, then put my arms through the spaghetti straps and adjusted the top. I glided my arms into the sleeves of the matching bolero top. My pretty painted nailed fingers secured the 12cm heeled (about 5 and a half inch) stiletto around my ankle. Shiny pink toenails peeked at me from under my sheer stockings.

Bracelets, necklace, choker, and long dangling earrings were placed. I put a bow that matched my dress in my hair and stepped over to the full-length mirror and checked my outfit while I sprayed perfume over me, under my dress, and on my legs. It was some sort of heaven I was in as I took myself in and ran my long, painted nails through my new hairstyle.

The gorgeous girl I always longed for and wanted to fuck was standing in front of me, and I couldn't help but throb incessantly in my panties. I sniffed the perfume on my wrists and let it fill me with femininity. I throbbed some more. Hmm, I wondered. I lifted my dress and slid my panties under my shaved balls, then lowered the dress again. Beneath the dress, my cock lifted and fell of its own accord, the tip rubbing the satin lining while I observed the dress in the mirror.

I throbbed more, knowing now I could wear the dress out just like I was and enjoy being free and no one would know I had a hard as rock cock under my dress. I walked around the room, looking down at the front of the dress. My cock bobbed, and the satin lining teased the tip, but nothing showed. I seated myself on the bed and crossed my legs. No problem. I pressed on my dress and could slide my cock between my thighs and bounce one foot. Yes! This was how I was going to go out.

Rising up and checking myself one more time in the mirror, I was overwhelmingly proud of what I had become. I was a gorgeous girl with a gorgeous cock and I was proud of it and it made me powerful and sexy. I was sure some girl would fall for me. At least I could talk with them and enjoy this incredible ambiance while I did it.

I slid my arms into the rabbit fur coat then cinched and tied the belt. My silver purse was at home over my shoulder, my thumb hooked on it. The glittery silver scarf wrapped around my neck. One last peek in the mirror and I heard Riley texting me. I took my phone from my purse. She parked downstairs.

I looked at my reflection one more time and couldn't help grabbing my cock through my dress and jerking it while I took myself in. The girl in the mirror was fucking hot and fucking was what I wanted to do with her; raise the hem of her dress up and stuff my cock into her, then she'd moan and beg for more. My mind saw a handsome guy fucking the girl in the mirror, but I was the girl. I was the hot sexy girl I always longed for and now I knew I begged to be longed for like she was. I had to leave, but couldn't stop. It was too good.

The satin lining slid on my hard cock as I jerked it. I saw the handsome guy behind me. His one hand on my shoulder and the other hand on my bottom under the dress. He was whispering in my ear. My breathing got choppy. My knees were weak. I whimpered.

5

"Hi, Riley!" Cassie beamed at me from the driver's seat; her sexy legs exposed and her cleavage showing from her open coat.

I was still a little flustered. "Hi, Cassie!"

"You seem nervous. Are you afraid of tonight?"

"Heck no. It's just that this is so intensely compelling. I mean, I almost..."

She was driving down the side-streets. "Almost what?"

"Uh...it's a little embarrassing. I mean. I'm so alluring and sexy that I... I uh...I almost came in my dress."

"I know what you mean." She laughed and touched my leg. "I'm hard as a rock in my panties right now. I almost wanted to have a good yank to get rid of it so I wouldn't be so distracted. But it all affects me so well, it would probably be back in a few minutes, anyway. I think it's a compliment for us. It's only natural for guys to get hot from sexy girls, right? Means we must be sexy."

My hand landed on her silky stockinged thigh, I squeezed it. "Right!" I laughed to break the tension and savored the sensation of her silky leg beneath my roaming palm, caressing it while gazing at her.

She slid her hand onto my leg and caressed me in the same way. "Very right. We are sexy, babe."

We drove along silently, my heart racing. I slid my hand further and further under her dress. She didn't stop me. "You know, Cassie, I pulled my panties under my globes so they could be free and it works. No one can tell and it's heavenly being free under the dress. It's liberating."

She glanced at me quickly, then back at the road. "Really? Wow! Seems I'll have to try that."

I slid my hand under her dress all the way and pulled her panties under her balls. "Let me get that for you." I pulled out her package and tugged her hard cock free, then gave it a few strokes before letting it go. I put her dress back over it, wrapped it around her cock, then stroked it. "See how silky the lining is? Isn't that delightful?"

She took a deep breath, concentrating on driving. "Oh god, it's lovely."

I stroked it, watching her face while I throbbed under my dress. I couldn't believe this was happening, but it was incredibly irresistible. "Am I doing that okay, sister? Is it enjoyable? Does it feel pretty?" I loved her hard cock in my hand. I loved seeing her react to me giving her pleasure.

She nodded hurriedly. "So pretty." Her voice was choppy. "Oh... god... too pretty.... huh!" She pushed my hand away.

"I'm sorry, Cassie! I didn't mean to upset you!"

She slid her hand on my leg, under my dress, and grabbed my cock and stroked it gently. "You didn't upset me. It was pretty alright. Pretty damn heavenly. Too heavenly. We need to find some girls before we go too far."

"Right. You're completely right. My mistake. I'll be a good girlfriend for you and behave." I pressed my hips up against her hand, letting her know I loved her hand on my cock.

She smiled and kept stroking me. "I'll behave too...as much as I can." She gave my cock a last squeeze and pulled alongside the curb, parking the car. She shut it off and leaned over with puckered lips.

I gave her a peck. "Don't want to mess your lipstick."

"It's twenty-four-hour, anyway." She grabbed my head and gave me a deep kiss, pulled back, and looked deep into my eyes. "God, this is *soo* bad. We may not need *any* girls... *girlfriend*." She put my hand on her cock and she grabbed mine. We kissed and stroked each other until we had to stop or make a mess. "Okay! Well... Let's go anyway and see if our plan works. If not, we have a Plan B now." She winked at me.

6

We slid out of the car into the blowing snow. It whipped and swirled around us; against our legs, under our dresses, and biting our toes. We tip toed through the inch or so on the ground, our bunny-fur coats wrapped tightly around us, taking tiny steps in our high heels, arm in arm to keep from falling.

On the porch, we stomped off the snow on our freezing feet as two girls arrived behind us doing the same. "I should have worn my boots and changed. My toes are freezing," one girl whimpered out in her tiny voice. We turned to see them. They were tiny to match the voices alright. About five foot five in four-inch heels and each of them around a size one or two with belted, camel-colored coats wrapped tight, revealing their tiny waists.

I smiled at them. "Hi! What a night for a party, huh?"

The blonde one beamed at me. "C'mon. Let's all get a drink" She took my arm and huddled close to me as the reddish blonde one grabbed Cassie in the same way and we made our way inside in minced steps in our heels, clicking away so incredibly erotically on the hardwood floors.

Inside, safe from the chill, her perfume wafted to my nose as she took her coat off to reveal a creamy, full and firm cleavage above a tiny waist. Her hips, under a body clinging sparky dress, spread above gossamer thin sheer stockings, sheathing shapely legs, perched atop tiny, strappy stilettos, revealing tiny pink toenails. My cock danced under my dress, thinking of how great it would be to fuck her tight pussy, as I shed my coat and she took it and hung it with hers.

She grasped my hand, as did the other girl with Riley, and we clicked our way like princesses to the bar. A young guy that didn't seem old enough to drink took our drink orders and mixed them while his eyes flitted about our cleavages.

My new friend said to me, "I'm Cathy, and this is my roommate, Jill."

I grasped her hand gently with my fingers and thumb. "I'm Riley and this is my best friend, Cassie. Mind if we hang with you girls tonight? Safety in numbers, right?"

"Sure, why not, right Jill?"

Jill leaned into us. "The more the merrier. Plenty of guys to fuck here." She laughed as she looked around at the nervous, well-dressed guys milling about, checking us out, sipping beers.

Our drinks arrived, and we clinked, then Jill said, "To getting laid, right, ladies?"

Riley and I nodded, and we all sipped the strong pink martinis. Jill motioned with her martini to us. "So you girls are nervous? Don't be. These guys are more nervous than we are. You won't need safety in numbers. As you can see, none of the guys have approached us yet. We all intimidate them. You know what I mean. Hot looking girls like you two."

I nodded. Cathy squeezed my hand and whispered to me. "Jill is really horny... all the time. I mean... I want to have fun tonight and possibly find a guy to enjoy sometime, but she's a little faster than I am. How about you? You want to get laid tonight?"

"Uh... I uh... I have my period."

"Oh, so you're on a tampon?"

I nodded.

"No problem. Me too. Just take it in your bottom. It's just as good, if not better, and you can never get pregnant. *IF* I find someone that sweeps me off my feet, I'd do that, period or not. I'm using a plug in my cleaned out bottom now. It's very nice."

"Ah... not sure if that's for me."

"Once you try it, you'll love it. You'll see."

Jill spoke up to us all. "Let's get a seat at that high top over there. There's four chairs around it." She grabbed Cathy's hand and dragged her, clicking away toward the table. We followed like two puppies, hand in hand. Jill and Cathy sat together, and I sat by Cathy, and Cassie by Jill. We all crossed our legs and hung our purses on the backs of the chairs.

The table had a charcuterie tray and other food. I took some of the kibble in the bowl and poured some in my palm. I nibbled and looked around. What if a guy came after us? These girls wanted guys. What if we told them we were girls with cocks, or they realized we were imposters? Could we fuck them? Would that work? Would they reject and expose us?

I felt a tiny hand gliding on my stockinged thigh. A tiny honey like voice said, "You seem nervous, Riley. Are you okay? Is this your first frat party?" Her hand glided sensually on my leg as she gazed lovingly into my eyes.

Oh god, did I want to *fuck* her. I'd jerked off a million times to pics of girls nowhere as cute, petite or sexy as her. I recrossed my leg, trapped my cock between my thighs, and bounced a foot, squeezing it delightfully with each bounce. "It is my first party. I mean... I never attended one all dressed up so sexy like this."

"Right. It's so much better this way, isn't it?"

"It is! It's so liberating and so sensual and feminine. Girls should dress like this every day."

She laughed and sipped her drink. "Sounds like something a guy would say."

"No no. I'm... I mean..."

"I know what you mean. It's sexy to dress this way; with the stockings and heels and being so revealed, vulnerable, and pretty. The walk high heels give a girl is so erotic too. It's all lovely to do, but so much preparation."

"Yes. Of course, anything worth anything always takes work. Cooking, school, work. Dressing pretty and feminine. Stepping prettily in heels."

"Are you an engineer or something? Life doesn't have to be work. Preparation isn't *always* work. It can be a pleasure."

"I am an engineer, actually. Or going to be. Trust me. Things that are worth anything take work. I guess you're right that preparation doesn't have to be work though. It was fun getting ready for this and the preparation and party were welcome and deserved after the semester I had."

"I'll bet. You poor girl, becoming an engineer. Hardly *any* girls do that."

"It'll be worth it."

"Most engineers are geeks and antisocial. You're not. Probably because you're a such a pretty girl."

"Thanks!"

She leaned in toward me and kissed my lips. "I'm glad we met. We'll make great girlfriends."

"I hope so. Can I get you another drink?" I reached for her martini glass, looking into her gorgeous, made-up, sparkling blue eyes.

"Please. Thanks, sweetie."

I looked over at Cassie, and she was engaged in conversation with Jill. Jill was being all touchy feely with her and I could tell Cassie was horny for her. This *could be* our night. If we didn't get beat up if our secret came out.

I clicked my way across the floor to the bar, my breasts jiggling and tugging on my chest, my hips swaying from each minced step, my hard cock sweeping the lining of my dress. It was as if I became alive for the first time in my life. I was enchanted, dreamy, powerful, sexy, confident.

The place was filling up, and there were definitely more girls than guys now. I put my foot on the bar rail and the cute bartender came over. "N'other martini, miss?"

"Two please." I handed the glasses to him and he dashed off.

A hand landed on my shoulder. "Hi, my name's Josh." A deep voice said in my ear. "Love your outfit. It's a really sexy dress."

Great! Getting hit on by a guy already. Shit! I was looking down into my purse digging for the small bottle of perfume and said, "My name's Riley." I took the perfume out, dabbed some on my wrists, and put it back. I turned to him. My heart raced off, my face flushed. "Hi... uh..." It was Josh from my project group. Shit!

"Riley? What a coincidence. I have a guy in my project group named Riley. Nice guy. Kinda a geek. You bear an odd resemblance to him. Somewhat sisterish. Not geekish like him, though. Really pretty compared to him."

I laughed nervously as his eyes flitted across my face and breasts. My heart pounded. "Thanks. I'd rather be called pretty than a geek. That's for sure."

The drinks arrived. "I have to take these back to my girlfriends. Talk to you later... uh... Josh?"

"Right. Josh. Later... *I hope*... Riley."

I stepped carefully in very tiny strides to not spill our martinis in their up-glasses. By the time I reached the table, I had calmed down a bit. My heart resumed a normal pace. Cassie caught my eyes, and I rolled mine at her, then she gave me a quizzical face. I shrugged and sat next to Cathy, who was chatting with Jill.

Cathy turned to me and smiled, taking her drink in her tiny, long, painted-nailed fingers. Jill stood and grabbed Cassie's drink glass and they both clicked away to get fresh drinks.

"Thank you, Riley. That was so sweet of you." She held her glass out and we clinked. "To both of us having a great night." She sipped and looked away, giving me time to check her out. She was bouncing a tiny high-heeled foot. I sipped my martini daintily while my eyes flitted her heaving, creamy breasts and her tiny nosed face, high cheekbones, raised eyebrows, and luscious, glossy-painted lips that would be *incredible* on my cock. My cock throbbed, begging for those lips around it while it stuffed into her pretty face.

She turned back to me and smiled. "Getting busy here."

Cathy wiggled her seat closer to mine. Her leg rubbed against mine in our stockings, her hand dove under the table, and glided on my thigh. The foot of my crossed leg bounced and made my cock, trapped in the dress's satin between my thighs, drool for her.

She gazed into my eyes. "Wait until later when we've all had a few drinks and they have their drawing."

"Drawing?"

"Yeah. For those that want a little more than just a conversation. You know... more than just a fleeting kiss or touch. They have a room for consensual gathering for more than touches or kisses, but need to have a drawing so there aren't too many people in there. It's big, but not that big."

"A room for what?"

"For people to get to know each other on a more... uh... intimate level. Petting, sucking cocks, fucking."

"Ah... I see. But there's a drawing, so not everyone gets to go."

"Right. And not everyone has to or wants to go. We'll be able to get tickets and probably all of us will get in. Don't worry." She slid her leg against mine and ran her hand up and down my thigh. "Us horny girls will get in. I can tell you're as horny as me and maybe even as horny as Jill. Right?"

My cock was throbbing uncontrollably. If I wasn't careful, I'd come right there in the lining of my dress. "Uh, yeah. I guess you pegged me. I'm *very* horny tonight. These clothes, all the pretty girls. Especially you."

"Oh! You like girls too? How nice. So do I." Her hand pressed between my legs, trying to get past my tight thighs. She took my hand and slipped it under her dress while she glanced around. She opened her legs and pressed my hand against her bare, shaved, wet slit. I gently slid two fingers into it and rubbed her clit.

"Oh yes. Riley, that's it. That's so good. That's why I like to wear crotchless panties, so this is easier. And... I lied. I don't have my period. I don't know why I said that even. I guess because I like it in the bottom best. So do the men because it's nice and tight. You never did that, huh?"

I shook my head, fingering her and looking into her eyes. She pressed her hand harder to get to my crotch. Should I let her? What would she do? "Uh...no..I never..."

I took my hand from her, wiped it on a napkin, then took my drink. I chugged it down.

Cathy laughed. "I think you need another one, girl! You won't get laid being that nervous. My turn." She tossed her drink down and took our glasses to the bar. She was quite the sight to see crossing the floor—like a tiny Barbie doll, her head swiveling and her face smiling at everyone, breasts jiggling with each step.

She chatted while waiting for our drinks. Then I got to watch her coming back toward me, carrying the martinis in tiny careful steps—a vision of feminine beauty and vulnerability.

"I'm back. Good thing too. The drawing is starting. Jill put all our names in it of course."

A guy in a black tie and tux came out to the center of the floor. "Can I have your attention!" He looked around. "Hello!"

Everyone quieted down. He smiled. "Everyone who put their name in for the more intimate meeting room where they can freely indulge in consensual behavior, is free to go in. There's no need for a drawing because the ticket count matches the capacity of the room perfectly. Go on in and enjoy! There's a bar in there too."

Cathy slid off her seat, slung her purse on her shoulder, and grabbed my hand. Looked like we were all off to the sex room. I walked holding her hand, my heart pounding, my breasts jiggling with each step, my cock throbbing and rubbing its tip under the satin lining. I needed to pee. "Cathy, can we go to the girls' room first?"

"Oh right. Good idea." She called out to Jill and Cassie and they came along with us.

After we got out of the stalls, I whispered to Cassie. "We need to leave. Josh is here and practically recognized me. Cathy want's to play with my pussy and teach me to be fucked in the ass and we're heading into a sex room where our secrets can be discovered by someone."

Cassie nodded and looked around then whispered. "I didn't get Jill's phone number yet. Did you get Cathy's at least?"

"Shit! No."

"Then we *can't* leave yet. I'm not passing these girls up. When we get their numbers, we can go."

Cathy came up behind me and grabbed my ass through my dress. "Hmm, cute bottom. The men will love stuffing that one."

7

We walked to the room holding hands. "Cathy, we need to exchange phone numbers."

"I know. Let's not forget, alright?" Her arm wrapped around my waist and she snuggled against me as we made our way. I was in heaven.

In the room, we refreshed our drinks and Cathy led us to a leather couch with end tables by it and seated us at one end. She drank half her drink and put it on the end table, then took my drink and placed it alongside. Leaning back and on the arm of the couch, she pulled me against her and whispered in my ear, "I have strap-ons at home you might like. I think you'd love me to use them with you." Her hand glided on my crossed legs, sending ripples of electricity through my body. There I was with a beautiful, tiny, sensual girl for the first time in my life and I had to be hiding a secret.

I kissed her deeply on the lips, slipping my hand under her dress and putting four fingers into her, my thumb on her clit. She gasped in my ear, her breath hot. "Oh yes, Riley. You're doing that perfect. Huh, uh…mmm, your thumb on my clit and all those fingers. Let me reciprocate. Please!"

"No honey. I have my period. Just relax and enjoy it." Her eyes gazed into mine, then roamed the room. I made her shudder, and she squeezed my arm tight. She whispered in my ear. "Very well done, Riley. That was the first one of the night. Mmm. Don't stop." Her leg twitched. She was incredibly responsive. I had to fuck her somehow, but my secret was getting in the way.

I looked around, and Jill and Cassie were in an embrace, kissing.

Someone seated themselves next to me. "Hi Riley. It's me Josh. Do you girls need any help?" He looked at my hand under Cathy's dress, my arm moving in and out under the hem of her dress.

Cathy poked me in the ribs and whispered. "He's cute! You should play with him." She looked up at him. "Sure. Have a seat next to Riley. I'm sure she'd be happy to entertain you."

Flustered, my hand still under her dress and inside of her, I whispered back to Cathy. "Help me, I don't know what to do. I never played with men. I like women like you." I discreetly took my hand from her and wiped it in the lining of her dress then brought it out.

She whispered back, "I like both. Perhaps you will too. Strap-ons are nice, but so is the real thing." Cathy leaned across me, put her hand on Josh's thigh and rubbed it. "Hi Josh. I'm Cathy." She stared at his hard cock in his pants. "How nice! Seems you're happy to see us." She reached out and rubbed his cock through his pants, looking in his eyes. "Why don't you let that beast free so we can entertain it?" She reached for his buckle.

He moved her hand away, unbuckled his pants, and unzipped them, then quickly pulled his perfectly shaved cock and balls out. It was huge and solid. "There we go. Meet my little friend, ladies." He smiled ear to ear and leaned back, putting his arm over my shoulder. His hard cock jerked of its own accord in the air.

I stared at his huge, perfectly shaped cock, unable to take my eyes off it. No wonder girls go for big guys like him instead of me. Cathy smiled an evil smile and said, "It sure is a handsome beast and so full of life." Cathy grasped my hand and used both her hands to wrap my fingers around his hot shaft, then squeezed my hands on it and forced me to stroke it while she smiled at Josh. "Riley's a little shy and sometimes needs some help to get started. Right Riley?"

I nodded, staring at my hand as if they were someone else's wrapped around that thick, long cock. Cathy let my hands go and caressed my legs. My brain said to let go of it, but my hands wouldn't let it go. I stared at it and continued to stroke it. It wasn't the least bit repulsive like I thought it might be. It was incredible to hold and stroke, knowing I was the one making him hard as a rock. I loved how hard and velvety it was and it was hard for me.

Josh whispered in my ear. "That's fantastic, Riley. Your hands are so soft and warm. Thanks. You're excellent at that. With you being such a pretty girl, and now knowing how good you make me feel, I'd probably be hard around you all the time... unless you helped me get rid of it."

I flashed a flat smile at him, then glanced back down. I could sense him watching me. Glancing at Cathy, she smiled, reached over to me and put her hand on my neck, pressing me down toward his cock. "Take it in your mouth for him, sister. I'll bet Josh would love your pretty face with that stuffing it."

A shudder shot through me, my cock leaping crazily under my dress. Josh was sliding his big hand on my leg, trying to get between them and under my dress. "Open up Riley and let me give you some pleasure, too." He pressed further. I stroked him faster and looked into his eyes. "Sorry. I have my period."

"No problem. If you want, I'd love to use your bottom."

Cathy poked me in the ribs. "Go ahead Riley. You'll love it."

GOD! What was I going to do? I couldn't let him find out my secret. To get his attention away from me, I *had* to make him *come*. Gawking at his cock, I stroked it with both hands.

My head inched closer until I could touch the tip with my tongue tentatively. I tasted his salty, somewhat sweet pre-cum. I took the head into my lips and ran my tongue around it. His body shuddered each time I passed over the hole. He groaned and said, "Oh god, take it all, Riley." His big hand gently urged my head down onto it.

I moved so I could see his face, my legs crossed and stretched to the floor, and slid between his legs. My jaw opened as wide as it could and I consumed it and experienced the velvety soft skin on my lips as he bobbed my head on it with both hands. He let my head go, and I kept bobbing my head on it, a hand stroking the lower portion of the shaft, and rolling his silky balls in my other hand. I lifted my eyes to gaze at him.

He was gazing down at me lovingly and petting my hair. "Gorgeous, Riley. It suits you so well. You're so pretty with a cock in your mouth." His hips lifted, and he began thrusting slightly into my face. I locked my eyes on his, savoring his reaction to me.

Cathy was massaging my legs and whispering words of encouragement telling me how good I was doing and how great it will be when I make him come. How empowered and desired and complimented I'll be.

I was in an alternate reality where I was a girl, and this was all normal. The empowerment and my ability to control his sensations and responses filled me with joy. The reactions from him were immensely gratifying and made me proud of the intensity of arousal I created in another person. I was on top of the world.

I flicked my tongue over the hole in his tip to make him shudder. Tugging and rolling his silky balls, I ran my tongue around his thick, silky shaft and tightened my lips against it, confirming his firm and sincere arousal.

He messaged his approaching fireworks when he put both his hands on my head and squeezed it. I could tell the performance I was giving him was phenomenal, and it exhilarated me to no end, being so successful at pleasing a person so well. My cock throbbed and drooled between my thighs in the satin of my dress and begged to come.

I became enamored with his cock. There was nothing else except me, his cock, and his balls. Mesmerized and fervent in my diligence about *making* him come for *me, I* wanted it... no; I *needed* it. Gobs of his salty sweet come were the rewards I needed, *knowing I* was the seductress that produced his *unavoidable* response to give his come to me because *I* was a gorgeous, talented, and diligent girl.

His hands clenched my head, fingers wrapped tightly in my hair, tugging it on my scalp. I gazed up to his eyes, looking down at me, his face distorted as he moaned and rolled his head on his shoulders to come back and have to look into my eyes again to see his cock dive in and out of my pretty face.

Suddenly, his legs tensed, his cock became like steel, his eyes burst open wide, and he gasped. His cock pulsed and the first gush ran across my hungry tongue. I guzzled it, bobbing my head on it and tugging on his balls. One after another, the gushes pulsed through my fist and past my tight lips into my mouth while I looked into his *oh so thankful* eyes.

I harvested his energy from him and consumed it as my reward. I was absorbing his passion into my whole body and my overwhelmed girl-cock responded by shooting come into the lining of my dress. My body shuddered and shook and I struggled to keep my legs together as my one foot in its high heel tapped autonomously against the floor over and over.

Josh's body fell limp. Still spewing my pent up passion in my dress, I continued to coax more come from him until he yanked my head off him while laughing. "Riley, my girl! You sure get into it don't you."

I lifted my mouth off his magic wand and sat up.

Cathy wiped come from my chin and fed it to me. "Waste not want not."

I licked her finger then tried to suck it as if it would feed me more. She giggled in her tiny voice.

I took a deep breath and had her hand me my drink from the table. I drank it down. Josh had put himself away and stood. "Thanks Riley. I hope I get to see you again. I mean, I hope you don't quit our project group." He turned to Cathy. "Nice meeting you, Cathy. Thanks for helping Riley get over her shyness. It was fantastic of you. This is who she's meant to be... A lovely, intelligent, beautiful, sexy, and *very* talented young woman."

"Nice meeting you, Josh. Glad you were the one to help her."

Cathy studied me, bouncing her leg and sipping her martini. My cock was going limp and my brain was telling me they totally fucked me up. I was exposed, ashamed. Josh knew exactly who I was. Did Cathy? I looked over to find Cassie. She was on top of Jill, fucking her on the carpet and there was a guy behind Cassie fucking her in the ass. She was thoroughly enjoying it. What had we done!?

Cathy wrapped an arm over my shoulder and caressed my leg. She clicked her nails on her phone, then showed it to me while a video played. "See how pretty you were taking care of Josh so well. You puckered your pretty painted lips and they wrapped so perfectly showing prettily around his cock. Your eyes were so bright and showed how much you loved doing it. Then, you swallowed it so well, too. This could be a porn video, girl."

I stared at the video of me relishing his cock in my face. Funny, I did look really pretty with his cock in my face, my painted lips slipping up and down his thick gorgeous shaft. My face was a face I'd fuck endlessly and forever.

"Are you okay, sweetie?" She rubbed my shoulder.

I nodded, watching the video intently. "Just need to sit here for a little while and rest."

8

Cathy snuggled to me, hugging my arm assuringly, her head on my shoulder. Her perfume wafted to my nostrils.

The video ended, and she put her phone away. "I'll send you the video, then delete it."

There was a slick wetness in my dress and I glanced down to see it wasn't showing through. I turned to Cathy. "Sorry about getting so crazy to not pay any attention to you, losing all control. I'm so ashamed for acting like I did."

"Oh Riley. Don't be silly. I could tell that was your first time doing that, and you enjoyed it as much as I did the first time. Did you come when he did? Your body shook."

I nodded sheepishly.

"So he's in your project group. That's good. You'll definitely see him again. I'm surprised he hadn't approached you before this."

"Well... I uh... This is the first time I've looked this good. I'm geeky normally." Should I tell her my secret? Does she know?

"I watched your partner, Cassie. Seems she had a *great* time. She fucked Jill and got fucked herself. She either had a strap-on under that dress or a nice cock." Her eyes roamed my face. The back of her hand caressed my cheek. "Neither of you have anything that would show you're males, but I have to ask... do you have those parts?"

I nodded sheepishly and looked around. "Please don't tell. Please? We thought we'd be able to meet girls better this way. I never thought about how to let a girl know I was a fake."

"Oh Cassie. You are *not* a fake. Just because you have something *special* and *wonderful* under your dress doesn't mean you *aren't* a girl. I'd *love* having a girlfriend like you. You have the best of both worlds. None of that stupid macho stuff. Plus, you're pretty as hell, *plus* you're a freakin' engineer, which means you're a genius practically."

"Wow. Thanks. So...it's okay that I spontaneously ejaculated in my dress while loving sucking a guy's long fat cock with immense fervor while dressing like a girl?"

She laughed. "Absolutely. I think it makes you even more interesting." She gave me a deep kiss on my lips, her tongue dancing in my mouth. "Mmm, I can still taste him on you, too. I think we need to spend more time together."

"Oh god. That would be fantastic!"

"About Cassie. Do you two have a thing together? I mean... are you committed?"

"We're close. I mean, we're fantastic friends, but we never had sex or anything before. Like I said, we did this dressing up to meet girls. That's all."

"You should stay this way. It suits you. You're a girl. You'll see." She smiled and ran her hand through my hair, her eyes bright with happiness. "A lovely girl." She grinned. "Uh, don't you think you should go wipe your dress off and freshen up? I'll take you to the girls' room."

I looked over at Jill and Cassie sitting and chatting. Jill had her arm around Cassie and Cassie snuggled next to her, glowing. Cathy pointed. "Seems your friend had a good night. You'll have to ask her how good it was. Then she can convince you of what you two are." She stood and put her hand out to me. "C'mon missy. Let's go clean your dress up and get you back in pretty girl mode. Be proud and happy about what you did. You should be glad for you *and* your friend."

I took her offered hand and stood. Jill stood, helped Cassie to her feet, and came over to follow us to the girls' room. Cassie leaned in toward me and whispered. "Oh my god, girl, that was incredible!"

"Did you get her number?"

"Shit. Not yet. You?"

"Me either. Let's not forget!"

I wiped off the moisture from the lining of my dress and used some damp paper towels to clean my sticky cock, then took a pee. I fixed my hair in the mirror, touched up my lipstick, put on perfume, straightened my dress, and adjusted my cleavage. Cassie was doing the same next to me and Jill wrapped her arms around Cassie and hugged her from behind, giggled, then fixed her hair, smiling in the mirror.

I turned to Cathy and gave her a big hug. I whimpered, "Thank you so much. Please... we need to exchange phone numbers."

"Of course. Relax. Don't get so emotional. Relax and just be the pretty girl." She took her phone out.

9

We clicked out way back into the consensual room with some Irish coffees and the four of us relaxed on the sofa together. Cassie and Jill were touchy feely and Jill actually seemed to be pretty smart and so did Cathy. All the while we sat there sipping and chatting, Cathy caressed my stockinged legs, snuggled next to me and I held her close with my arm wrapped around her petite body. I was in heaven.

Cathy's hand slipped further and further up my thigh to my crotch. "So... are you filled with prettiness again, sweetie?"

"Beautiful. Very feminine and happy, and I think I'm falling in love." I gave her a peck on the lips.

"Good girl! That makes me thrilled because I think I am too." She broke free of my arm and swung herself around to sit on my thighs, facing me. She lifted her dress and scooted forward, her hand under it. Tiny fingers wrapped round my again hard cock. "Oh, how nice," her tiny voice whispered in my ear.

She lifted herself up and guided my cock into her tight, wet, hot pussy. Her eyes opened wide, and she giggled. "It's so fulfilling." She clenched down on it over and over while I lightly held her hips, our dresses covering us bunched up between us. She lowered her top and let her breasts free. I used both hands to massage them and suck her nipples while she clenched and unclenched my cock, then lifted slightly and lowered herself back down. I whimpered around her nipple.

She leaned back and gazed lovingly at me while she administered her therapy. "See how well a pretty girl like you fits with a pretty girl like me?"

"Oh god yes." I glanced at Jill, who was now doing the same to Cassie. We had done it. We were going to come in two hot girls.

Success! Our plan had worked. Now everything was worth every bit of effort and emotional trauma.

I leaned back and took her all in. I placed my hands on her hips and lifted my hips to shove my cock into her. She shuddered and squeezed her nipples, then her body tensed. Her eyes popped open, and she assessed the look on my face and my actions. I whispered. "Cathy, are you ready for it?"

She scrambled off me like I was filth. "Sorry. You can't come in me... yet. That'll happen... possibly... at the next party this week." She snuggled next to me and wrapped my dress around my cock and stroked it. Jill soon scrambled off Cassie and reseated herself next to her. The girls readjusted their clothing and picked up their Irish coffees. They both smiled at us.

We waited. "Were they teasing us? Why did they do that?"

I spoke up. "We have rubbers, if that's the problem."

Jill shook her head. "Sorry ladies. No... that isn't the problem. We're both on the pill and clean as you both are. You can come in us anytime.... except right now, or until you become the girls you are, completely."

I tilted my head. I looked at Cathy and she nodded and said, "Jill will text you both instructions on what you need to do to prepare for the next holiday party at the Sigma Beta Gamma frat. Until that party, neither of you is allowed to orgasm. You can do whatever you want except orgasm. Jerk off, suck each other's cocks... anything, but you are not allowed to come. Got it?"

We nodded sheepishly.

Jill nodded. "Good. Now, right now, I want you both to wrap your cocks in your pretty dresses and jerk them for us, but don't come."

I looked at Cassie. Jill took Cassie's hand and made her do it while Cathy did the same to me.

Jill nodded approval and patted Cassie's leg. "Good girls, now imagine doing what we did earlier with you girls and imagine finishing inside of us."

We both started jerking off faster.

"Don't you come!"

I let it go, and it bobbed under the dress. I took a deep breath. "How long do we have to wait? What do we have to do?"

"Keep staying on the edge. Then follow the instructions I send to both of you tomorrow morning. Got it?"

"Got it."

Cassie nodded, her face blank, still mindlessly stroking herself through her dress.

Jill and Cathy stood and offered their hands to us. We stood, they led us to our coats, and we all hugged and made promises to them to follow their instructions then we all left.

10

Cassie stayed at my place since it seemed stupid to be out driving in this snow more than needed. Not to mention, we didn't have any reservations about sleeping in the same bed anymore.

Cassie borrowed a cute merry widow lingerie set from me with sheer black stay up lace-top stockings and I wore a short satin slip with matching panties that had garters on them that attached to sheer black stockings. I put some feathered black mules on my side of the bed for when I got up and we slid under my satin sheets.

I was still hard from earlier. "This is difficult, Cassie. All I want to do is come."

"I know. Your satin sheets aren't helping either. They're so nice slipping against my legs." She slid her legs around, brushing against mine, then slid a foot on my leg. "Oh god."

I slid my leg over hers and rubbed her with it. She had a longing face. I checked the clock. "We'll never get to sleep."

"I know. What's worse? Disobeying or not sleeping for a few days. Plus. We'll be crazy at the Sigma Gamma Beta party and we know what their parties are for."

"Yeah. They say it means Sigma is summation, Gamma is for girls and Beta is for boys, so the summation of girls and boys, which is sex. Remember, we had to sign the consensual sex waiver when we entered last time? They don't have just one room. It's the whole place."

"Yeah. A lot of good it did us. There were no girls left for us and we left."

"Right. But now we *are* the girls."

"Right. Hmm. I don't know if that's good or bad right now."

"So Cassie, you got fucked in the ass."

"Oh my god, yes. It was heavenly and to top it off, I was in Jill, too. I didn't really notice Jill though as much as that cock in my ass. He penetrated my soul so damn well. Instead of being a violation like I thought it might be, it was being connected to him by having him deep inside of me. His passionate energy flowed from his cock into me like a transfusion of his lust. As far as with Jill went, I was just laying there with my cock moving inside her every time he shoved it into me. He was the better part of it. You have to try it. Want me to fuck you? Your cock doesn't even need to be touched and we'll both come from it. "

"Really? Come from just being fucked?"

"Like I said. You'd never guess how fantastic it is being so connected to someone and having their cock pulsing and spewing their passion into your soul. Let me do it to you."

"Not now. I need to get used to the idea."

"Not sure how if you don't try it."

I rolled over, wrapped my arms around Cassie, and kissed her deeply. I slid my hand into her panties and stroked her lovely cock while I humped her leg. "You have a very nice cock, Cassie."

"Thanks. Your cock is nice on my leg."

"Thanks."

Cassie massaged my breasts. "Aren't these wonderful? I don't want to be without them."

"Mmm, its wonderful to have you do that too."

Cassie's other hand slid into my panties and we both humped into each other's hands. Cassie nibbled my ear lobe then whispered, "You know... we could suck each other off now that we both enjoy sucking."

"But we'd be disobeying."

"They don't expect us to obey. They know we'll go crazy if we do. We can *try* not to come, though. We just have to slow down or stop for a while."

I slid around and took her cock into my mouth at the same time she took mine. We started a pattern of running our tongues around the shaft, flicking the tip, bobbing our heads on the shafts and tugging balls gently. We did it in time together as if music was playing and repeated the pattern over and over. My heart was racing. I yanked my cock from her face and let it bob in the air. She did the same. She laughed. "That was close."

"Mmm, deliciously close. Ready?"

We both dove back on and indulged in each other again. My whole body tingled from the level of arousal I had. I loved having Cassie's cock in my mouth. Finally, I could give something to my best friend that we'd both cherish. I wrapped my arms around her hips; her crossed legs squirting her cock and balls out to me tightly. She did the same to me, giving me a hug.

We hugged tight and sucked and bobbed and ran our tongues around each others shaft and suddenly her cock swelled rigid as did mine and both our cocks pulsed as we shot come into each other's face, swallowing it greedily, our bodies shaking and us two girls whimpering around each other's cocks. It seemed like forever before it ended and we lay there limp and spent with each other's cocks in our mouths, catching our breath and letting them go soft.

Her cock was still in my mouth when I was almost asleep. I licked it off tenderly and pulled her panties up over it, then slid back up to her. I spooned her and cradled her in my arms and fell fast asleep.

11

In the morning, I slid out of bed, went pee and took a shower. When I came out, I slid into a short pink robe and my feathered mules and clicked into the kitchen. Cassie had breakfast made, standing in her cute nightclothes, wearing heels and finishing frying the bacon. I wrapped my arms around her from behind and gave her a hug. "Morning, sweetie."

"Morning. Thanks for doing this... Letting me stay over and stuff. We should just live together and save some money."

"True. Let's plan on it."

We sat to eat and dug in like prisoners who had been on an eating strike. Our phones dinged at the same time. We both stopped and grabbed them. We read it. Cassie shrugged, put it down, and went back to eating.

"Did you read that?" I asked.

"Yup. Sounds fine to me. They even told us where to buy the stuff. Jill said they bought them for themselves some time ago."

"A clean out for the shower? Eww!"

"Relax. It makes sense. Then there's no chance of messiness when Josh or any other guys fuck you."

"Oh, my god. This is nuts."

"Riley! You have to try it. Do you want Cathy as a girlfriend or not? She wants you to do this. Didn't she say you couldn't come in her till you did?"

"You came in Jill already."

"I was a big girl and got fucked in my pretty bottom. You're a little girl that is being silly. We're doing it or I won't move in with you either."

"Cassie."

"I mean it. Grow up. We're doing the dishes, running out to get the stuff, then coming home and following the instructions. The party is coming soon. I don't want any whining from you. Grow up Riley. You're a receptacle for men's passions now." She grinned and nodded. Sipped her OJ. "And maybe....if you're lucky...my passions. You already were one with your mouth. This is even better."

Dishes done, Cassie showered, and I dressed in a brown corduroy miniskirt with a heavy, cream-colored, V-neck sweater, brown tights, and gold suede, wedge-heel boots. I checked myself in the mirror and when Cassie came out, I did my hair and makeup. I loved my new hair and how I looked in daytime makeup. It was so much better than just thin eyeliner and a dab of mascara. My eyes popped and lips looked luscious.

Even though I was only semi hard, I was immersed in the wonderfully feminine and at home in my new skin. Every time I thought of having something in my butt, I'd lose all libido. But it still was better to be a non-horny girl than the fem boy I used to be.

I spritzed some perfume on and stepped out to the bedroom where Cassie was admiring herself in the mirror, wearing a maroon leather miniskirt that came to just above the knees where black high-heeled boots met it. She topped it off with a pink V-neck sweater. She sprayed perfume on and put her earrings in.

"You look lovely, Cassie."

"Thanks. And only twenty bucks for everything I'm wearing. Thank god for Goodwill stores and the Salvation Army." She turned to me and took me in. She walked over and gave me a peck on the cheek. "We only need one shower attachment now that we're moving in. Let's go get the stuff."

I drove my car, this time relishing my high heels on the pedals and my skirt around my legs and my silky stockinged legs against the leather seat. It had stopped snowing, and it was sunny and gorgeous. The roads were clear and the air as fresh as towels on the clothesline.

Cassie slid her hand on my leg while I drove and I rested my hand on top of hers as she did. "I love this Cassie. I love you."

"Same same, sister."

I pulled into the adult toy store. It was pretty seedy, as most of them are. We ran in together. A decent-looking guy smiled at us from the counter. "Can I help you, ladies?"

Cassie clicked straight over to him, took her phone from her purse, and showed him Jill's text and said, "We need two of everything except the shower attachment." He read it, nodded, and went into the store from behind the counter. He trotted from place to place and came back. "All set. You sure you don't want to look around?"

"Sorry. Maybe next time. We're on a tight schedule today."

"K." He rang it up. I paid for it and we left and drove home.

We helped each other put the shower attachment on, then washed the other things and set them on the counter in the bathroom. I stared at them like they were aliens.

"Riley, don't look so scared. Now take your clothes off, take a poop, get in the shower and clean out your butt. Then I'll do mine and we can put our plugs in. I'll put batteries in them both and get them ready with the lube on the bed. I can't wait."

"I can. I'm not looking forward to it."

"Not yet. You will, though. Just get the tasks off the list right now. It's all you need to do. Remember, Cathy wants this from you. Go!"

"What if we just got married and I can forget about Cathy?"

Cassie shook her head and laughed. She slapped my ass. "And you think I won't want to poke that pretty ass of yours? You'll still need to learn this lesson. This is like calculus for engineers. You can't be an engineer if you don't know calculus. Calculus may not be pleasant for everyone to learn. This may not be. But once you've mastered it, a whole new world opens up to you and all the rewards come in."

I shook my head and scoffed. "Yeah, someone *coming inside* my *ass* is the reward they get."

"Exactly! And trust me. It's your reward too for being so enticing to them." She slapped my ass hard. "Go, girl!"

12

I did as instructed and it wasn't half as bad as I thought. It actually was nice after. I came out to Cassie, and she got in. I put on my clothes again so we could go out later. Cassie was out in a few minutes, smiling. "That was refreshing! I feel so damn clean now." She had her robe on. I sat on the bed looking at her, my legs and arms crossed.

"Don't give me that look. The clean out was nice, wasn't it?"

I shrugged. "I'm not putting my cock in a cage. That's ridiculous."

"Okay then. We won't cage. But it'll be pretty darn hard to keep from coming without it. Especially plugged with a vibrating inflatable plug. You'll want to wank it all the time."

"Stop talking about it."

"Okay then. No cage. Now the fun part is you need to be aroused for the plug to go in easily. If not, you'll fight it."

She knelt on the floor before me. "Lift that skirt, girl."

I lifted it and pulled my panties aside. Cassie took my limp dick in her mouth and looked up at me while she sucked it and tugged it with her lips. She looked gorgeous doing that. My pretty girlfriend reached under her robe and jerked her cock with one hand while sucking me and looking up at me. It was so pretty to watch her; I got hard immediately. Her eyes opened wide, and she popped off it and stroked it, smiling up at me. "That was fast. I like you responding to me like that."

"I couldn't help it. You're too pretty with my cock in your face."

She laughed and sucked it intently again, looking up at me while jerking herself. Just as I was about to come, she stopped.

"Okay, on the floor on all fours, and put your head down on your forearms and your ass in the air. He's going in!"

I groaned and did as she asked, my cock bobbing in the cool air, begging to come. I stroked it slowly to keep the riding the edge sensation going.

The cool wet tip of the plug passed my butt-cheeks and pressed against my hole. She pressed it and it stretched me a bit.

"How's that, Riley?"

"Kinda good, actually." I pressed back against it, then rocked against it, sensing it go deeper each time. Then, suddenly, it sucked in to the hilt. I gasped and gave a little squeal.

"Good girl, Riley. It's in." She turned on the vibrations and adjusted them for an intense bursting on and off. It was nearly silent. She pumped the plug up and it began to expand and grow longer inside of me. The bigger and longer it got, the better the sensation, and then a vibration would send a ripple of pleasure into me. I humped back against it until it seemed it shouldn't go any larger. "Okay, stop."

She set the plug and took the hose off. She patted my bottom. "Go walk around and see if it's okay."

I did, and it was heavenly. I imagined I was a gorgeous woman sitting on a gorgeous cock. "Oh, my god! This is good. A real cock feels this good?"

"Better. A person and their passion are in you. You feel their soul."

"Fuck!" I straightened my clothes and took a deep breath. "My phone will control it, right?"

"Right. Pair it on bluetooth."

I took my phone out and adjusted the vibrations to make it more bearable and not drive me so crazy. I sat down, wriggled on it, and smiled up at Cassie. "Good to go. You're next."

She stood before me, her hard cock held between her finger and thumb, offering it to me. I leaned down and sucked it until she was ready to come, then I put her plug in. She stood and walked around. "Good enough." She took her phone and adjusted it, then put her clothes back on.

13

Cassie dressed again in her pink top and maroon leather miniskirt and boots. She was spraying perfume on in the full-length mirror. "We need to move my stuff over here. I might have to be selective about what to bring to save space, huh?"

"Nah. We can get some of those stack hangers and hang some clothes in the front closet where there's lots of room." I sat there rigid in my panties, wriggling a bit on the plug. "This is distracting."

She was playing with her phone and wagging her hips. "It's great though, isn't it? Oh, god... Mmm."

She put her phone in her purse, came over to me, and gave me a light kiss on the lips then rubbed my cock through my skirt. "Yes, great. Just like the way you feel right now to me, Riley."

"K hot stuff. Let's get this move done at least part of the way, so you don't have to keep running back and forth. Then we can go out to lunch somewhere."

"Good idea."

We drove to Cassie's. Packed a bunch of stuff in the car, brought it back, and put it away. We were productive and satisfied, but the problem was we were horny as hell and so much so, we were oozing.

I put my coat on and slung my purse. "I'm hungry. You?"

"Sure am, sister. Hungry for a cock in my ass shooting lots of come in it. Ready for me in your ass?" She walked over seductively.

"We're supposed to obey. Maybe we should have cages on."

"See? Told ya." She rubbed my cock through my skirt. I tugged her to me, crushed our breasts together, and lifted one leg, pressing it against her cock while I humped her leg. We kissed deeply.

"Oh god, Riley. Please fuck me, please?"

I imagined being in Cassie's tight ass. It sounded so good. I wriggled my ass, the plug shot off another round, and I imagined Cassie fucking me. I was approaching the point of no return and broke our kiss and embrace and stood there oozing into my panties with one leg twitching, looking desperately into Cassie's eyes and said, "We can't! We have days yet. Let's go eat. Damn those girls. Damn Cathy!"

I held her coat for her while she put it on, took her hand, and dragged her out to my car. We stepped through the wet snow in the sunshine. I was glad we had our boots on. After letting her in, I started the car and brushed it off. I climbed in the car.

"Cassie, I see what you mean about cleaning off a car in a skirt in the wind, even if it isn't snowing." I sat and buckled my seat belt. Cassie's hand landed softly on my leg. "I want to fuck you."

"I know. I think I want it too, but we're not allowed. Should turn down the vibrations on the plugs? It'll make it less urgent."

"Yeah. I guess."

We turned them off, and it was still enticing and begged for more. "I want it back on, but I don't. It's good like this. I sure wish we could get the monkey off our backs and just enjoy being us for a while. I hate the girls are making us do this."

At that moment, my phone rang. I took it from my purse and answered it. "Cathy! Hi!"

"Hi Riley! Good to hear your voice. Have you two bought your things?" I put her on speaker.

"We sure have and we're wearing the plugs now, but not the cages. We're horny as hell and don't know if we can last until the party, even if we put on cages. Last night we couldn't take it and so we cheated and sucked each other off in a 69 then fell asleep. This is brutal." I looked at Cassie who was listening and nodding. Her eyes flitted about my face. They went to my breasts and back to my lips.

"Riley, I have to apologize to you and Cassie for Jill. She just wants you two to experience everything and not be limited now that you've chosen to be girls. I agree with that, but not with her methods. How is it having something in your pretty bottom now, honey? Is it pleasant or not?"

"Oh god. Yes, it's great. I'm ready to get fucked, and Cassie has been begging me to let her be my first."

Cathy's tiny voice howled and yipped. "Oh, my god! That's great! What in the world are you two waiting for? Don't worry about Jill. She'll be happy you both know how good a cock in the ass can be."

"Really? Seriously? You won't hate me and Jill won't hate Cassie?"

"Of course not. My suggestion is this. This new world of yours has much more to explore in being the girls you are than just sex. So get your rocks off and get the sex out of the way and then be the girls you are without the sex. Enjoy the rest of it. Plan and prepare for the party day. Go do things."

"Wanna join us?"

"I can't and Jill's tied up with family stuff too, but for sure we'll see you at the Sig Gamma Betta if that works. You girls have plenty to ponder like, if the guy that fucked Cassie is what she wants, or if Josh is what you want, or if I'm still the one you want, or maybe now that you two are more intimate and can be that way, maybe it's the two of you that are together. Riley, I don't mind if you aren't exclusive to me, but if you are, that's good, too. We're all too young to be committing to just one thing. That's why I was insistent that you suck Josh's cock and have love made to you in your bottom so you can try new things. Who knows where we'll end up after we graduate and who knows what we'll want? We need to explore, right? College is for learning."

"Oh, my god Cathy. Even though you sound and look like a little girl, you are brilliant! Thank you."

Cassie yelled to her. "Thank you, Cathy. I love you!"

She laughed. "Okay ladies. Now whatever you're doing, Stop it and go take those plugs out and Cassie, make love to Riley."

14

As we ran back to the apartment, we held hands like two young lovers. We slammed the door behind us, ran into the bathroom, took our plugs out, washed them, then put them away. We kicked off our boots, climbed on the bed, and fell into an embrace, our hands going directly to each other's cocks as we kissed deeply.

"Oh god, Riley. I never could imagine us having this together. I've always loved you."

I stroked her hard cock tenderly and gazed into her eyes. "Me either. I never imagined I would ever have sex with you, never mind want you to put your pretty cock in my bottom. I want it there now."

Rolling on my back, I shimmied to the head of the bed, then pulled my skirt up and my legs back. Riley tore off my panties and ripped my tights from the cutout crotch. She lifted her skirt and guided her substantial cock toward me. I watched as she pressed the head against my lubed ass.

She looked into my eyes. "Ready, girl? Ready to have your first cock?" "Oh, yes... please, Cassie." I wriggled my bottom closer to it, looking down. She placed the tip against the hole and I wriggled against it. It filled and spread me deliciously. I looked into her eyes and pulled her hips to me. "Fuck me, honey."

Cassie looked into my eyes as she moved it ever deeper. I rolled my head on my shoulders then focused on her made-up eyes. "Fuck me, girl!'

She thrusted fiercely, and quickly, whimpering as she did. My cock flailed in the air between us, a drop flying off it now and then. I watched her cock go in and out of me, then grabbed her breasts in my hands and pressed them against her. She reached a hand up and squeezed my breast, looking into my eyes and thrusting.

The sensations going through me flowed from head to toe. My cock seemed so hard it would burst and my leg twitched and my feet dangled in the air. I grabbed her tight ass and urged her faster and harder while glaring into her eyes. "Fuck me. Your cock feels so good! Fuck me, girl!"

She put her whole effort into it, making the bed shake and my body slip on the sheets. She pinned my thighs back tight to the bed and held me fixed while she rammed her beautiful cock in and out. I could see from her face and hear from her whimpers she was as close as I was.

"Come inside of me, Cassie. *Please* come inside me. I'm ready to burst."

She grunted, whimpered, then stiffened her whole body, her legs shooting back from her as she pressed herself deep into me as if it would come out of my mouth. Her body shuddered, and her cock pulsed inside of me as it dumped the first load of her come into me. My cock shot off a spurt that hit my face, and she pulled out and rammed me repeatedly. My cock flailed in the air, come flying off of it.

Cassie collapsed on top of me as she gasped for air. I held her close and stroked her hair. I wiggled my bottom on her softening cock and kissed her neck. "That was wonderful, my love. Incredibly wonderful." I hugged her tight.

She peppered my face with kisses and lifted herself up on her elbows. "It was. It was heaven." She kissed my lips and thrusted her cock a few more wonderful times, then removed it. She sat on the edge of the bed, still catching her breath. I sat beside her and put my arm around her. "This is incredible. No more monkey."

"It is. two relaxed girls. Let's get lunch and then I want to get some skinny jeans and long tops to cover my cock that'll show in them so I can wear jeans and boots and for protection from the cold. And I want a new casual, not bunny fur, coat, so we don't stick out so much."

"Good idea. Sometimes a girl just need to wear pants."

15

Lunch, Goodwill, Salvation Army, wash and dry the new clothes and we finished our tasks for the day. We both changed into some jeans and boots with long drop cowl-neck sweaters with V-neck camisoles under it. The outfit was good; normal, relaxed, not sexual and demanding.

My phone rang. I took it from my purse. "It's Josh. We aren't supposed to meet over break." I answered it. "Hi Josh." I put it on speaker and put in my new earrings while I listened.

"Hi Riley. I hope I didn't get you at a bad time."

"Nope. No problem. Always there for the project team."

"Good. I was hoping you's say that because I'd like to get the group together for a quick update so we can hit the road running after break. I don't want any blips."

"An update?" I sprayed perfume on, then combed my hair in the mirror.

"Yeah. You know. I think you know you'll be like you are after break, right? I *hope* you'll be. You know. Like you were at the frat party. You'll be a girl, right?"

"Uh... I think so. I mean... well."

I looked at Cassie. She nodded and whispered in my ear. "I'm not changing back, and I doubt you will. This is a good idea."

"Right. I'm a girl now. So you wanna get the team together?"

"Yeah. I want to introduce you while you're out of the room and then have you come in and have them meet the new you. I think it would be the easiest way for everyone to deal with the change. Can we?"

"Uh... sure... when?"

"In half an hour?"

I looked at Cassie, and she nodded.

"Works for me. Can I bring my new roommate? She moved in with me this week. Her name's Cassie."

"Oh sure. No problem. Wasn't she with you at the frat?"

"Yeah. She was. We're best friends and now we decided to save some rent and live together since we're both girls now."

"Okay if I introduce her too? You know...as having done what you did?"

"Sure. Some of them probably know her since she's in engineering, too. That would be a good way to break the ice."

"Great. See you both in a little."

I put my phone in my purse. "Ready, Cassie?"

"Ready as ever."

Cassie drove, and I relaxed, looking out the short drive to campus. We meet in the mechanical engineering building. I texted Josh, and he had us wait down the hall until everyone was there.

We stood, nervously taking in the typical familiar smells of school. You know, how schools always seem to have that smell. Not bad, not good, just a smell that brings back memories of tests you thought you'd fail or seeing your grade on the board in the hall. My phone went off. Josh texted me to come in.

We clomped our new chunky, high-heeled boots over our skinny jeans with our long, open, camel hair coats to the door. I looked at Cassie as I held the knob. "This is it. Ready?"

"Ready."

I could hear Josh talking, so I waited, and we listened through the door.

"The person who I want to honor today is a team member you all have the utmost respect for. They've helped all of us when we were stuck and needed help. That person isn't here right now, but will be, and you probably know who I'm talking about. It's someone we all thought was different but who we respected immensely. I'd like you all to re-welcome our friend and ally, Riley!"

I opened the door, and we walked in. It was dead silent as I looked around the room and waved a little wave with my fake-long-painted-nailed fingers. "Hi everyone!"

Their eyes all burst wide and smiles crossed their faces as they began to applaud and cheer. Josh walked around, handing out beers to everyone. I pulled Cassie next to me. "You may know my roommate, another engineer... Please welcome Cassie too, in her new look."

Another round of applause and everyone stood from their seats and surrounded us, patting us on the back and telling us how good we looked and how happy they were for us to have the courage to do it. We took beers from Josh and we all chatted in a group.

It astounded me how welcome and accepting they were of us. We got offers to go to dinner that we turned down and some of them said how fantastic we looked and how sexy we were. I guess educated people can be like that and these guys were definitely well educated with superior cognitive abilities. They weren't all geeks like us, or femboys like we were, but they were all very cool now, even the ones I used to think were macho brutes.

We sipped our beers and enjoyed the company, then they all left. Josh held the door for us. "Did I do okay? Was it a good idea?"

I looked up at him and tugged on his coat, pulling him close to me. I looked into his eyes. "You are a scholar and a gentleman. Thank you." I blew him a kiss.

His face turned red. "Gosh. Thanks." He laughed. "Can I take you girls to dinner?"

"Uh..." I looked at Cassie.

She shrugged. "I think we'd just like to have a chill night, the two of us. Thanks for the offer, though. Will you be at Sigma Gamma Beta for the holiday party?"

"For sure. You two? Say yes. Please say yes." His eyes were bright with anticipation. It made me blush.

"Uh..." I laughed. I was going already, but he didn't know that for sure, even though I asked him. "We're thinking about it. We need to plan our outfits and it's so much preparation."

He laughed. "You know anything worth having or doing takes work. I know you don't care about the effort. My guess is you'll be there since you asked me if I was going, so now that I know that, I'll be there for sure and I hope we get to spend some time together." He glanced at Cassie. She smiled and nodded and said, "You *have* to go. We'll be there looking for you."

"Super!" He reached into his coat pocket, took out an envelope, and handed it to me. "This is from the group. While we were having the beers, I walked around and got donations for you to build your new wardrobe."

I held it and looked at it. "Really? No, I can't take this."

"You have to. Everyone wanted to help. You've given everyone so much, they wanted to help you in your new presentation."

I looked at Cassie. "Don't look at me. You know you need it. Take it. It's wonderful!"

Josh said, "Open it."

I opened the card. It was a thank-you card and everyone signed it. They filled it with cash.

Josh said, "I counted it. Four hundred and twenty bucks." He smiled and put a hand on my shoulder. "Go shopping."

He motioned for us to leave as he held the door. We walked out hand in hand. "See you at the frat, ladies!" He locked the door and walked down the hall the other way.

We looked at each other. I checked the time on my watch. "Wow. This is great. I'm in the mood for pizza and beer. You?"

"Sure." Cassie took my arm in hers and we left down the hall to go to a bar.

We sat at the bar and ordered a loaded pizza with two long drafts. When we were sipping and chatting about the party coming up and what to wear, Cathy and Jill showed up. We had plenty to tell them about, and they were both happy for us.

Cathy rubbed my shoulder and said, "You two should go get dresses for the party with that money. Have fun. Do it up. Right Jill?"

Jill leaned across Cassie, her hand on Cassie's thigh. "For sure. This is the event of the year. We should go shopping together tomorrow. Get you some really hot outfits. Whadaya say, ladies?"

I shrugged and looked at Cassie. "We have no plans, right?"

"Right. We'll go."

Jill patted Cassie, and Cathy patted my thigh. We had a couple of beers together. Jill was getting fucked in the ladies' room when I peed, of course, and Cathy just chilled with us. It was a great night with our new friends who happened to be girls. How weird.

We stood outside; the snow falling peacefully as Jill dug in her purse, looking for her keys and dropping unopened condoms on the ground that Cassie quickly picked up for her. After she found her keys, we all hugged and said goodnight.

Cassie and I arrived at home, changed into some sexy nightclothes, cuddled and snuggled then played and caressed and finally sucked each other off and fell to sleep, looking forward to what the next couple days would bring.

16

In the morning, the two lovely girls we were took their time jerking each other off in bed, then showered together and got ready to go shopping with the other girls. I wanted to wear dress shoes so I could see how a dress would look with them. I peeked out the window, and it was snowing. "Darn. It's snowing again, and I wanted to wear dress shoes to try on dresses."

"Take them in a bag. We have bags. No one will mind."

"Right." I found a pair and packed them, then put them by my purse. Put on a bra and my gel breast forms and a camisole and low cowl neck sweater. Adjusted my cleavage, then put on sheer pantyhose to try the dress on with, and slid a tight pair of stretchy panties on to tuck my dick in well. I shimmied into my tight skinny jeans and slid on my boots.

Cassie had dressed similarly, and we quickly did makeup, perfume, and jewelry and were off to meet the girls for breakfast.

We all ate and had fun talking about the party to come and Jill filled us in on just how wild it has gotten before. "Anything goes there, girls. Don't be bashful. You sign a waver entering, you know."

I nodded and sipped my coffee. "I know we've gone before. Had no luck with the girls, though. But we saw what went on."

Jill grinned, then sipped her coffee and said, "Did you see guys with their dicks in cages and girls with their pussies exposed? I wore a dress with the front cut up and crotchless panties one year. It was awesome. Got fucked lots. Those poor guys in cages, though." She laughed. "They wanted to get fucked, but ended up taking the cages off and sucked each other off. I should have brought a strap-on for them."

I shook my head. "Guess we didn't stay long enough to see that. It was pretty depressing when there weren't enough girls and none of them paid any attention to us, so we left."

"They will this year. Everyone will. We'll help you pick magnificent dresses for it." She winked.

Cathy grinned. She chuckled a tiny chuckle. "I'm not sure you two are ready for this. It can be overwhelming. It's good. Don't get me wrong. But so you know, I sucked at least six or seven cocks last year. I was DP'd twice." She laughed. Then gazed up at the ceiling. "I was sore for a week." She rubbed my leg under the table and looked at me. "Ready Riley? Are you in for it?"

I raised my eyebrows. Was I? It sounded intense, and I was enjoying not having a monkey on my back and acting like an insatiable slut. I loved Cassie and our ways of satisfying each other so we could enjoy being girls *without* libidos. "I don't know. Cassie?" I squeezed her hand.

She shook her head. "*Honey*, you promised Josh already. We both did. I'm sure there will be people there just to be with us. It doesn't have to be overwhelming, right Cathy?"

"That's what I thought, but when you get going... it takes over. It's good though. Not a bad thing. A great way to start a new year for sure. Lots of wild memories."

Jill chimed in. "Just do it, you sissies! You'll love it. Now let's go get you two some outfits!"

17

It was fantastic being out with these girls, shopping together and trying on dresses. Jill was very picky though, and we found nothing until we hit a store with really feminine, almost bridal like, very short, layered, lace overlay, crinoline dresses with corseted waists and cleavage revealing V-neck tops. They were really cute and came in an array of pastels and white.

Cathy held a white one up against me. "Try this one on." I took it from her and inspected it while she dug through the other white ones. "Oh there! My size!" She took it out and put it under her arm. "And one for Jill." She turned to Jill. "Want to try it on?"

"Nope. I already have my outfit. Thanks."

Cassie was watching her. "I'm the same size as Riley. I hope there's another."

"I know, sweetie." She slid them across the rack, checking the tags. "Got it!" She handed it to Cassie. "Let's go try them on."

We all went into the changing rooms and put on our dress shoes and the dresses and came back out where Jill waited for us. She stood from the chair and covered her mouth while she chortled. "You all look incredible. We can make a theme out of this. You'll all be virgin brides! I love it! Do you girls like them? We can do sheer white stockings and garter belts, sheer white panties, and I can even slap together some quick bridal veils to wear. And none of you will even need bras with them, even for your forms, girls, and you'll all have touchable bare shoulders."

She walked around us, observing us as we took turns looking in the three-way mirror. She lifted the hem of my dress and felt the material, then looked closely at the sewing and fabric. "Hmm... I think I can really make you girls into the center of attention with these." She tugged on the corset ribbons on my back, adjusting them and pulling my waist in. "This is fabulous. When you take them off, I can take them home and make sure the ribbons for the corset stay in the holes and are easy to cinch.... along with a couple of other modifications to make you girls easier to use, too."

Cathy was looking at herself in the mirror, lifting the hem up and down. "Seems pretty easy to get to things as it is. What are you thinking of?"

"Oh, nothing big. Let's just buy them and I'll take them home and make matching veils and do the tweaks. Tomorrow, you girls can all come to my house and we'll all get ready together. Sound good?"

We all looked at each other and shrugged and nodded. I smiled at Jill for being so nice to offer and do all this. "Sounds great. Thank you so much. I'll buy the dresses with the money I told you about. Okay?"

"Sounds great. Lets find garter belts and stockings and some fetishy high stiletto bridal heels. I think those things are at the other end of the store. Sound good? Ready to be brides?"

Cathy snuggled next to me, then pulled Cassie to her with her other arm and wrapped her arms around us. In her tiny voice, she said, "I can't *wait* to be with my fellow brides in various acts of *consummation.*" She giggled and covered her mouth.

We all found what we needed and went home. Jill with all our packages to do her magic.

18

Cassie and I drove out for Japanese together and had some sake and tea and a lovely light dinner. We got home, slipped into some night slips and silky robes and turned on the tube, snuggled on the couch under an afghan, and watched a chick flick.

Cassie's hand roamed to my panties and slid inside. She wrapped her soft warm hand around my cock and slowly, gently, lusciously stroked it. "Hmm, seems you're a little spunky, princess."

"Yeah. A little. It's tempered with my nervousness for tomorrow. I mean, I'm excited as hell to be wearing that bridal dress but worried about all the attention we might get." I glided my hand into her panties and around her sweet cock, and did the same for her. I looked into her pretty eyes.

She winked at me. "Don't worry. I read the rules. The waiver is to say we're consensual, but only as long as we want to be. If anyone says no, it's no, and that's that. Remember Cathy and Jill had turned guys down there before with no issues. People were respectful even if they were all horned up."

"Yeah. I guess. I heard that too. I don't know. I guess it'll be fun. We'll have a wild girls' night out night to remember forever."

"That's for sure." Our attention drifted back to the movie. A guy was making love to a woman. "That looks beautiful, doesn't it?" I stroked her faster as she did for me. "Mmm, having him filling you. I always wondered how that must be for a woman and now I have a pretty good idea. There's nothing like being penetrated and filled. His passion is tangible in you. Mmm." She stroked me faster. "Hmm, I sure could use that guy right now."

"Really? Well, I have something I can use for that. But I can't do it unless you let go of it." I kissed her on the cheek and grinned.

She flipped onto all fours on the couch and lifted her satin covered butt in the air. I took the lube we put on the end table just in case we wanted it to jerk with and coated my dick. I got behind her and pressed it through her cheeks and against her hole.

"Oh yeah, Riley. Fuck Cassie, your sissy girl."

She pushed back against it and I slid all the way in and she gasped. "Oh god, Cassie. You're so fucking tight and hot. You should see how good this looks from behind. Your shapely butt cheeks are so nice and seeing a cock going into them is incredible." I held her hips and pumped her hard. "We never did this from behind."

"From behind is like a dirty slut and I love it." She pressed back against me in time. "You have to try this. Not seeing who's behind you is an odd turn on too."

I grabbed her hair and wrapped my fingers in it tightly so it tugged on her scalp.

"Oh god yes. Take me like a beast. Use me like a blowup doll."

I fucked her hard and fast, yanking her head back with her hair with one hand on her ass. I slapped her bottom a few times.

"Oh, yeah Riley. Fix this bad girl."

I slapped her bottom until it was pink, then took that hand and wrapped it around her neck, squeezing it some while tugging her hair. I quietly yelled at her in my very girlish voice, "Take my cock, you sissy bitch!"

She laughed. "Oh, my! It's a girl behind me! Fuck me harder, little girl!"

I fucked her and tugged her hair and squeezed her neck and watched my cock going in and out of her. I shoved it hard and deep, getting a gasp out of her and held it there. Letting her neck go, I reached around, wrapping my fingers around her oozing cock and squeezed it and stroked it while I dumped my load into her while whimpering.

She whimpered and came in my hand voluminously and when I finished ramming her a few more times, my come leaking around my cock, she collapsed on her belly and I fell out and on top of her. I peppered her face with kisses.

We rolled over, wrapped our legs around each other, and embraced, our breasts pressing firmly together, and kissed deeply. I broke the kiss to catch my breath and breath the perfume in her hair. "Mmmm...luscious...magnificent....life is better than good...it's fantastic."

We snuggled, laying on the couch together, and fell asleep watching that woman getting fucked by her other boyfriend.

19

It was heavenly waking up on the couch wrapped in each other. I peeked with one eye at the clock above the TV. It was 8 AM. We had slept for ten hours. I pulled my arm from under Cassie and stretched. She let out a cute little groan. I stroked her hair. "Rise and shine, pretty girl. We have a big day and night ahead of us."

She slid up, and we sat next to each other, looking out the window at the flurries. She rubbed my bare thigh. "I slept really well. We'll have plenty of energy for the party." Her hand slid to my panties and rubbed my limp dick. "But she's still sleeping? Should I let her?"

"Nah. Wake the bitch up. She needs to do her morning duty, so I don't have that monkey in my panties all day."

She wrapped her fingers around it and tugged. I grabbed her cock and stroked. I hardened. "Mmm, lovely way to start the day." We slid around and moved our cocks together and Cassie wrapped her hand around both of them and we humped against each other's cock into her hand.

Cassie gazed into my eyes while we humped. "You know, sweetie. I was just thinking. We shouldn't come this morning, but just edge on and off all day. I want to be really hard under that pretty dress, so sexuality infuses me. I mean, that dress would be incredible to wear even without a hard-on. It would still infuse me with femininity, prettiness, and the longing, receiving spirit of a bride, but it'll really fill out our sensuality if our libido is higher. Then, it'll be delectable… fill our every cell." She humped her cock against mine in her hand and her breath became choppy and she let out a little whimper.

I rolled my eyes and whined. Humping together. "But I want to come on your cock."

She humped a couple of more times and let our cocks go to bob free. "Sorry, we need a modicum of self-control now so we can lose it later. You know I'm right."

"As usual. Every engineer I know is always right." I kissed her lips, and we got up to make breakfast, our cocks tucked back into our panties.

We ate and did dishes and sucked each other to the edge then we showered and shaved the little of hair we had on our bodies and soaped each other's cocks to the edge then we loofah'd each other and dried each other off and skin creamed each other, then skin creamed our cocks to the edge then we did our hair and tried different up do's and wraps to look more bridal and virginal. We put some light makeup on for the day.

We redid our fingernail and toenail polish and sipped tea while it dried, then watched our pretty painted fingers bring each other to the edge again. "Oh god, Cassie. This is too much. I need a break. I think my libido is high enough."

Cassie checked her watch. "It's lunchtime. Let's grab a bite to eat at the sub shop and then we can pack our bags to go to Jill's. I think we should pack for overnight so we have something other than our wedding dresses to wear if we get stuck somewhere in the snow and have to stay over."

"Oh right! I forgot there's a storm coming. Did you check the weather on when and how much?"

"After 8 PM and 12 inches."

"At least everyone will make it to the party. They may not leave, though. I'll drive, so we have four-wheel drive at least."

"For sure. We can bring our big shoulder purses for our overnight and still use our beaded purses for the party."

"Right."

We packed, went to lunch, killed some time in the mall, buying long open finger white lace gloves for us and Cathy and by then it was time to go to Jill's. I put her address in maps and hit go. I turned to Cassie and put my hand on hers. "Ready sister? Ready for this? Are we sure we want to do this? I'm not hard right now thinking about it."

"Hell yes, we're going! When you put that dress on, you'll get hard. Don't worry that pretty head. Then when you see Josh's cock, you being dressed as a sexy bride ready to get fucked, you'll be really hard." She laughed.

I drove off, optimistic about our evening to come...to come...and to come again. Hopefully.

20

Jill's house was a large Victorian nestled in alongside a huge frat house. "Wow. She has a magnificent house. Right next to a frat though? Too bad that's not the frat we're going to tonight. We could just walk there."

Cassie laughed. "Jill probably picked this house based on having plenty of cocks close by."

"For sure. I think she might be a nymphomaniac. Poor thing."

"Well, it's a night like tonight we may wish we were more like her. I'm still not hard. Too nervous."

"Me too."

We parked the car, and trudged through the six inches of snow left uncleared from last night, up the steps and to the porch. We stomped our boots off and rang the bell. The door opened instantly with a beaming Cathy to run out and hug us both. "I'm so excited for you girls! Wait until, you see what Jill's done for us with the dresses and veils and panties and other stuff."

She led us in and hung our bunny coats. We followed her into the kitchen. Jill was pouring tea. "Hello ladies. Some tea?"

I clicked up to her in my heels and kissed her cheek. "Hello, Jill. Sure."

We sat at the big table in the kitchen, blew on the steaming tea, and snacked on some butter cookies while it cooled. Jill had bottles of pills on the table with no labels. Odd.

She talked about what she did for us making special panties out of sheer white with lace ones that she added sheer, stretchy, open tip ball and cock sheaths made from an extra pair of white stockings, and how she had ribbons to tie our balls and cocks up to stand out under the dress. Then she described the veils. No problem with libido now. I was getting aroused hearing about all that.

I slapped the table. "Oh, hey! I forgot. We bought stretch-lace, open fingertip gloves for the brides too."

Jill slapped the table. "Perfect! I was thinking about that being missing. Good job, ladies."

We sipped our tea, all of us getting more and more excited by the minute. I was staring at the pill bottles.

Jill said, "Don't worry. I'm not addicted to drugs or anything and these are for all of us. The white ones increase libido, the green ones keep you hard and keep cocks from ejaculating. Women it doesn't affect like that and they still have multiple orgasms. Cathy knows. She takes them too and the green ones make your clit really responsive."

Cathy nodded excitedly, put her tea down, and swallowed. "I was taking them the other night at the frat. Remember how sensitive I was when you were fingering me, Riley?"

"Oh yeah. You came so fast."

Jill went on, "And the orange ones are to allow you special girls to come when it's time. It lets the ejaculation process happen. Until then, you're just hard as hell and super horny. You'll be begging to come but it won't trigger." She chuckled. "Ready to take some? They're perfectly safe. No fancy drugs or addictive things in them. I promise."

Cassie and I looked at each other. Cassie's eyes went wide. "Hell yeah. Have a guaranteed hard on as long as we want until we want it to end? Sounds fantastic! Riley was worried our libidos wouldn't be any good with us being nervous tonight. This fixes it. Right Riley?"

I looked at Cathy with a blank face.

"Don't be scared, princess. Trust us. I told you I've taken them. Jill takes them. It's all good. You'll enjoy yourself more this way and be less nervous. Do it for me?" She rubbed my leg and gazed into my eyes, head down, eyes up, a pout on her lips.

I rolled my eyes. "Okay already!"

Jill opened the bottle of white ones first. "They're all candy coated, but don't chew them. They'll taste awful. Just swallow them." She handed one out to each of us then put six of them in front of each of us. "For later."

We all swallowed the first one down.

She gave us the green ones. We swallowed them down, and she put six of them in front of us. She put the orange ones in her purse. "I'll hold these for now. Put the rest in your party purses along with your rubbers and things."

We did. What were we in for? I became aroused and hard. It was incredible. Was it from the anticipation of dressing in that feminine, sexy bride outfit, or was it from the pills? Heck. It didn't matter. I wanted to get changed into a bride. There was something especially exciting about that ultra feminine outfit theme. Maybe because a bride always gets laid by her man. Maybe because I wanted to believe I was girl, and I really wanted a man. Maybe it was the way the dress accented my breasts and legs and I was all in virginal white.

I had to stop thinking about the why and just go with the wonderful effect it had on me. "Can we dress now? I can't wait anymore. I want to experience the prettiness and femininity of that bridal outfit and *be* a bride. *Please?*"

21

Jill led Cassie, Cathy, and me to a large room upstairs where our things were all laid out on a king-sized bed. Cassie and I took our bridal shoes out of our bags, put them on the bed, and laid the gloves on it.

Cathy took us into the bathroom and helped us with our makeup and hair while she did hers. When we were done, we were the vision of young brides with finely finished makeup, contoured, and lipsticked with cupid's bows with pouty lips and eyes that popped and drew one in to see our obvious joy inside.

We hurried into the bedroom and stripped naked. Cathy's petite little perfectly shaped body was a thing to behold. While I slid the shimmery, sheer white stockings up my legs, my cock jumping constantly, I watched her dress. I attached the silky sheer white stockings to the white satin and lace garter belt with the four clasps on each leg. I slid the baby blue garters up to the tops of the white thigh highs. I slid the modified sheer and lace panties up, and slid the snug, silky sheath over my hard cock, leaving the tip sticking out.

I wrapped the stretchy lace ribbons around my globes and then over my cock and back around under my globes then over my cock again and tied a bow, lifting it all up and out. I stared at my bobbing cock. It looked splendid so proudly displayed and dancing. It felt *soo* damn good. Those pills must have worked. I looked around for my purse and took another white one and green one and swallowed them.

Cassie laughed. "Was wonderin' when you'd do that. Cathy and I already did." She stood like a goddess in the fetishy high, strappy, white beaded shoes we'd all wear while she tucked her gel breast forms in her top and made cleavage; her cock rigid and gorgeous in its gossamer sheath.

Cathy went over to her and knelt down to adjust Cassie's sheath so it was smooth and then did her ribbons for her and tied a bow above her cock. "How pretty. Now that *is* a very feminine and *pretty* cock. I love the contrast of cock with satin and lace. It seems so right. A balance of the masculine and feminine." She kissed the tip and licked the hole. "Mmm." She giggled and stood up.

My dress was up and forms in. Jill came into the room. "How's it going, ladies?"

Jill wore a sheer, black with black dots, see through body suit with stilettos like ours, but in black. A very short, sheer, black skirt, belted with a wide, leather, studded belt, held the skirt draped over her perfect butt and barely covering her crotch, which had a sheer overlap in the bodysuit for it (which I could see her shaved pussy under) from front to back allowing instant access to her available depositories. She wore a sheer bolero that stopped at the edge of her breasts showing her hard nipples with silver nooses attached to a silver necklace, which wrapped around her neck when it came out of her top. A choker was wrapped on her neck that read, "LUV to FUK & SUK". (I guess just in case somebody didn't pick that up from her outfit.)

Her makeup was intense and her nails long and glossy black. Silver bracelets, rings, and ankle bracelet completed her outfit. She smelled heavenly and powerful. I was stuck with my mouth open, taking her in while my cock danced under my dress.

She clicked her petite body over to me and slapped my ass with her tiny hand. "What are you staring at young lady?"

"Uh... uh... shit... Jill, you look boiling hot. Love how you pulled back your reddish hair and how you fluffed it behind you. It's intense... Like your makeup is." I looked her up and down. "And the see thru... the see thru... not many women could pull it off, but it's so sexy on you and being able to see your pussy is incredible. It looks great too."

"I put some hot pink twenty-four-hour lipstick on the folds to make them show better. Thanks for the compliments." She looked me up and down and lifted my dress. "Nice. I see the pills are working well. Hey! Wait! I know what." She knelt down and took a tube of lipstick from her belt pouch. "It's the hot pink twenty-four-hour stuff." She grabbed my cock firmly and tugged it. She wiped the ooze off with her fingertip and painted the head with the lipstick over and over until it was bright pink metallic. "There! Wag it in the air until it dries good. Come here Cassie!"

Holding my dress up, I played with my cock happily wagging it like instructed. Jill did Cassie's cock next. She admired her work then put her lipstick back in her purse and stood. She looked at all of us. Cassie and I were wagging our cocks and our eyes were taking in Jill and Cathy while our mouths hung open.

Jill laughed. "Okay, you too. I think it's dry so you can stop playing with yourselves... if you want. Okay. I think we're all ready... oops... almost." She took the veils and attached them firmly in our hair with a clip she had sewn into them. She draped them around our shoulders.

She had me stand facing the full-length mirror and found an edge on the front of my dress and tore off a cut-out she made in front with a ripping sound.

"Hey! Jill!" I whined.

"Shush. It can go back on."

She turned me around and did the back. Open arches in front and back exposed me. My cock was leaping, it's pretty pink head proud and attracting the eye. I turned to look at my bottom and there was a perfectly placed opening in the sheer back of the panty that gave easy access to *my* depository.

I turned back and forth, checking myself out. I was *fucking enticing as* hell and extr*emely* fuckable. "Wow. This is incredible. I can't believe you did all this. I can put it back in place to go out?"

"Yup. It'll stay put too. I learned to do this stuff when I couldn't find clothes to fit the way I wanted to, or wanted to wear something different. It's like a hobby. I'll put it back on for you so can take it off when you want to." She turned to the others. "Yours are the same."

Cathy came over and gave her a kiss. "Thank you *soo* much."

Jill nodded and smiled and checked us out again. She fixed my dress. "Where are the white lace fingerless gloves?" She looked around seeing them on the bed and we picked them up and stretched them up to our elbows. She nodded approval. "Perfect brides ready for consummation."

She took a white pill from her belt pouch and swallowed it, then took a green one. "Probably had enough of these already, but what the heck. I love being a horny slut that can't stop coming." She laughed.

We all hurriedly took another white and green.

22

We all put on our coats and changed into our boots, taking our shoes in our overnight purses. It was snowing like hell out already.

Cassie whined. "This snow wasn't supposed to start until 8PM! I hope it doesn't stop people from going."

Jill chuckled. "Didn't stop anyone in past years. Animal motivations come from deep within. Ain't nothin' stopping them. You girls have four-wheel, right? If not, you can ride with us."

I nodded. "We're good. I have new tires and four-wheel. We need to get moving though before it gets too deep." I wrapped the bunny coat tightly around me and cinched the belt snug. I put the collar up, loving the caress of the fur on my neck and chin. Cathy came over and tucked our veils into our collars and we did the same for her.

We all checked each other out to see we were ready to enter the blowing snow. Jill took a deep breath, hugging her night bag tightly to her. "Let's do it!" She opened the door, and we all ran out to our cars.

I used the fob to unlock it and let Cassie in then I tossed her the keys and grabbed the brush and brushed the back window off. The snow was blowing against my lightly clad legs sending chills through me. The car started, I hopped in the driver's seat, and shut the door. "Holy Shit! I hope we can see the sides of the roads."

Cassie was setting defrosters up then she buckled her seat belt and put her hand on my exposed thigh and squeezed it. "You're good in snow. I'm not worried and I'm still hard as a rock under this dress. The icy snow blowing under it even felt sexy. I think those pills worked."

23

I was glad this was one of the nicer frats. The house was vast and impeccably restored. We ran up the porch stairs and clomped our boots off.

The door opened for us. Christmas decorations abounded. "Hurry, get inside before you freeze," said the cute, smiling, young guy, who looked like he could be sixteen, but I know he wasn't or he couldn't be there. He was wearing a butler's tux with his zipper down and cock and balls out, held firm by a black silicone cock and ball ring with a bow tie tied behind the head of his rigid dick.

I glanced at it and laughed then smiled at him. "Cute! I like it. Very classy too with his little bow tie. Like you! Cute and classy."

He flashed his brilliant teeth, his eyes bright and fresh. "Thanks! That's the reaction I was hoping for. Maybe we can spend some time together later. My name's Ben." He helped me with my coat.

"Thanks Ben. I certainly hope so. My name's, Riley."

He nodded and said, "Okay later hopefully, Riley. Now show me your college IDs so I know you're of the age of consent, then you'll sign a sheet in the book on the table. Print your name then sign. Just like the example I used of mine that's showing in front of it." He helped the others take their coats off and hang them up then checked our IDs. We all printed and signed.

We slung our purses on us and walked past the old grandfather clock in the foyer, our heels clicking on the hardwood floor. The place already had quite a few people there. There were girls with whips in dom outfits, some cute girls with their cock's showing under their prissy sissy outfits, another bride, some hunks of guys wearing just an open shirt with shiny metallic bikini underwear revealing their huge hard cocks under them. There was a nurse, a sexy witch, a sexy Santa, and elves in tights. Most of them revealing their sexual arousal in one way or another. The erotic energy flowing was palpable.

My cock danced under my dress as we walked in minced steps over to the bar; Cathy and Cassie draped on each of my arms. With each step my breasts jiggled deliciously, tugging on my chest. We all took a seat and ordered martinis.

I crossed my legs and bounced a high-heeled foot, toes pointed, looking around the room. Cathy slid her hand on my stockinged thigh and whispered. "Too wild for you?"

"Nah. Been here before, remember?"

"Yeah, but you didn't last."

"I'm much better this year. A sexy and confident girl ready to play. Versus a boring, mundane femboy nervous as hell."

"Good girl." She patted my leg and gave me a peck on the lips. "Me too."

Our drinks arrived. Jill toasted. "To being satisfied beyond belief." We all clinked and sipped.

Jill turned to the tall guy next to her, seated at the bar with a huge exposed cock and started talking to him. She took a sip of her drink then stroked his cock with her tiny hand.

I looked around. Josh saw me and came over with a smile ear to ear. "My, how great! You're all dressed for our wedding ceremony tonight."

I grinned. "Thanks but... aren't you being a bit presumptive?" I gave him a peck on the lips.

"Don't worry. I'm not ready for that. But we could consummate a marriage of minds and bodies tonight. Ours." He ran his hand over my bare shoulders, sending a warm, loving energy through them. "Your shoulders are so pretty." My cock danced under my dress.

"Thanks. Consummation sounds nice. May...be...we will." I looked down at his crotch. He was wearing a black thong with a tuxedo front with a hole in it, which lifted his shaved cock and balls. He was half hard. I stared at it. "He seems a bit depressed."

I reached out and took it between my thumb and forefinger then lifted his heavy meat and dropped it. "Hmm." I stared at it. It soon became rigid and stood straight up.

He sipped his drink. "Better?"

"Much. It looks so handsome dressed up in its tuxedo when his posture is good."

"Thanks." He moved closer and put his arm around my shoulders. "You know, I was thinking. You're aware I have a web company, right?"

"Yeah. A successful one too. I always wondered why you were still in college."

"Right. I just know the more I know, the better off I'll be at being *more* successful. But my point isn't about that. You see, I bought a big old frat house and I've been refurbishing it. I have tons of space and I was thinking you and Cassie should stay there and save money on rent. Then, you could have more money for the girl things I'm sure you'll be needing to get. A woman's wardrobe is much more diverse than a guy's. The rooms have lots of closet space too. I redid one of the big rooms with a walk-in and attached bath. You two could stay in that suite. No charge for rent. Whadaya think?"

Cassie was listening. She leaned in. "Let's do it! We're tripping over our clothes right now trying to figure out how to manage them. Riley, please?" She shook my arm looking in my eyes.

I turned to Cathy. "Did you hear Josh? What do you think?"

She laughed. "We live right next door to Josh. I think that would be great. He has the big frat house next door to Jill's place."

I turned to Josh. "Alpha Omega is yours?"

"Yup. Never took the sign down. Low on the priority list. They moved because they didn't have the money to do the repairs and fix it up. I got it for a steal. C'mon. We'll move you in tomorrow. Weather permitting of course."

I took a deep breath and looked into his bright eyes. A guy that not only wasn't repulsed, but seemed to have a crush on a girl like me, and being right next door to Cathy and Jill. Wow. "We'll do it. Thanks!" I put my hand out to him.

He took it and squeezed my limp hand. "Fantastic. It's a magnificent house to study in too. It's so big and there are tons of friendly spaces that are real quiet."

"Great. Okay now let's have a party." I gulped down my drink and pushed it forward for a refill. I took out another white and green pill and downed them. Josh looked at me confused. I handed him one of each. He popped them in his mouth and smiled. "Nice. Thanks."

I scanned the room. Jill was moving around. She had a guy that looked like he was ready to fuck her against the wall. Cathy had slid off her seat and was making her way to a guy coming into the room. He was a big handsome black guy with glistening, hairless skin on his chest and arms and a huge shaved cock and balls sticking out of his black dress pants. He smiled ear to ear, and she tore off the front and back of her dress like a stripper as she approached him. She leapt up into his arms. She straddled his waist and quickly pulled his cock into her. He held her up by her bottom like a doll and thrusted up into her.

My drink arrived. I took it and held it to Josh. "To tonight."

"To tonight." I stood and undid the front and back of my dress. Cassie had already done that and was on her knees in front of a couch, sucking a cock, and jerking hers. I took Josh by the hand. "Let's find a nice place where I can indulge in devouring that wonderful cock of yours for a while. No coming though."

"If you say so."

I clicked in my heels, carrying my drink and leading him by the hand. My cock flailed in the air with each step and my breasts jiggled. I walked in tiny minced steps immersed in the petite, feminine, pretty, and sexy girl I was. My veil fluttered on my shoulders reminding me I was a bride. I squeezed Josh's big hand in mine as we turned into a large dining room where I seated him on the table and took a seat before him, gazing up into his eyes. "Ready for me?"

He wagged his cock at me grinning. "What does this say? I want to see it in your pretty face."

I flipped the veil over my face. I slid the chair closer and used both silky, lace covered hands to gently tease and caress the length of his cock while looking up through the veil at him. "It's so velvety and big." I ran a finger on the underside and rolled his balls in my palm. I glided my silky gloves over it repeatedly.

I squeezed it tight with both hands and stroked it. Through the veil, I stared at it. I could imagine being a bride and doing this on her wedding night. I could practically taste and feel his cock in my mouth and began to drool. My cock leapt up and down beneath the table.

I flipped my veil back and dined on his cock. I rolled his shaved balls with one lace covered hand while the other stroked his base and my mouth stretched to take the top part in. Racing my tongue around his shaft, I flicked his tip and bobbed my head, all the while looking up into his eyes to see his reactions.

I loved seeing the pleasure in his eyes. I brought him to the edge, even though there shouldn't have been an edge to fall off after the green pill he took. But I was careful not to push it. I savored his cock for quite a while as my body tingled all over and I rode the edge of release. It was great knowing I wouldn't come and ruin my motivation.

When I started to get a sore back and neck, I slid alongside of him on the table and gave him a hug and kiss. I stroked his cock. "Sorry, my neck was getting sore."

"That's okay. Maybe you just need a new position. I love the tailoring of your dress." His hand glided on my thigh. It grabbed my cock and stroked me in little strokes. "How would you feel about letting me deep inside of you, miss?" He squeezed my breasts and his tongue ran circles on my neck, his breath hot, his cologne filling my senses.

"Mmm. I'd feel flattered. Sounds lovely." I looked around then grabbed his hand and led him out of the dining room. Where did I want to get fucked? We drifted back into the room with the bar and walked past people doing everything. Cathy was being fucked on a couch by that big handsome black guy. Jill on a table. Cassie was on her knees on a pillow busy servicing three cocks, all standing erect around her.

I led him through the room, my cock head bright pink and proud ahead of me, taking tiny steps in my heels, holding my veiled bride's head high and being proud as I led my man. Not knowing where I was going, I found a staircase at the end. We climbed it. At the top of the stairs was the hallway. There was a barrier halfway down the hall but there were three rooms open before it. There were signs on each. "Please keep the rooms clean for others to use." I peeked inside of one. Slick, black satin sheets and pillowcases on a king sized bed. Josh laid on the bed. I took some lube out of my purse and rubbed it on my hole.

I slid onto the bed, scurrying my way back to the head and spread my legs with my arms out to him. "Josh, you don't have anything do you? I want you to take me bareback." I was so glad I learned how to clean out for this occasion.

"Nope. I'm clean." He rolled over and slid between my legs and I pulled him toward me then guided his cock to my begging hole. He pressed it with the tip and I wriggled against it, forcing it to stretch me out. It seemed he'd rip me in half for a moment and then he made it in. I gasped. "Keep going." He prodded it along while looking into my eyes.

"That's it Josh. Keep pushing. I want it all."

He thrusted slowly, each time going a little deeper until he finally had it all the way in. I wriggled my ass on it, bottoming it into me. "Oh god yes, Josh. Your passion's filling my body with tingles and joy. *Fuck me* with that gorgeous cock. Fuck your bride and come inside me."

Josh grasped my thighs and pressed them back onto the bed to secure me. I looked into his eyes as my feet in their high heels pointed to the sky and flailed in the air by my head with each thrust. He stroked it the full length, getting faster and harder as time passed.

He was breathing deeply as he used his might holding me to the bed and fucking me from bottom to throat. His eyes locked on mine. "God it's so good to be a part of you like this, being deep inside of you. Is it good for you, my pretty bride?"

I nodded, biting my lip, my head rolling on my shoulders, absorbed by the sensations. I wanted to come, but I didn't. Thank god for the green pills. Oh shit! Maybe Josh won't be able to come. He had to. I needed it.

"Are you coming, baby? Please come for me."

He grunted and shoved and pounded me. "It's so good! You're so tight and I love being connected to you like this."

I lay there prodding him on. Squeezing his ass. Urging him on. Then, suddenly, he moaned and cried out, "Oh god, Riley." His body stiffened, and his cock became totally rigid in me and then it pulsed. It shot gush after gush into me. I hugged him tight to me. "That's it, baby. Fill your bride with your come."

My body was in a state of bliss, electrified all over. My toes pointed in my heels, my cock oozed but didn't shoot. It was as if I started to come but just stayed at the beginning of release as it oozed down my shaft. Josh pumped every bit of come from his sweet cock into me then collapsed beside me, catching his breath. I stroked his hair and lay there in wonder of it all.

How could I have been missing this all my life? He wrapped his arms around the pillow and closed his eyes as I lay there. Stroking my cock through its silky sheath I felt the wetness from the oozing he had made it give. Staring up at the ceiling, stroking myself slowly, I rested. I ran my hand over my silky legs while jerking my cock then I squeezed my breasts. I lifted my head and flipped the veil over my face enjoying the thought of being a bride freshly fucked. Josh was quietly resting, or maybe sleeping, next to me.

I turned to the side. Cathy was there holding the hand of the young guy that took our coats, Ben. He was smiling down at me. Cathy held her finger to her lips. "Shh." She motioned for me to follow her.

I slid off the bed quietly and followed them. She took us to a room where there were three more cute guys like Ben. All standing there smiling with their cocks out with little bow ties on them.

Cathy knelt on the floor before them and pulled me down with her. We both took their ties off and dove onto their cute cocks. They weren't tiny, but not huge either, but attached to really cute guys. I got the impression looking into their eyes while I sucked they might be a bit like Cassie and me.

We enjoyed their cocks thoroughly then Cathy dug in the purse on her shoulder and took out four "Sure Fit Snug" condoms and handed them to the boys. They quickly undid them and put them on while Cathy brought me over to the couch.

She laid on it, pulled me on top of her, and guided my cock into her. Ben grasped my hips and guided his cock into me. He fucked me like a rabbit, making cute little squeaking sounds and shoving me into Cathy while she stroked my hair and gazed into my eyes. "Isn't this lovely? You're so pretty."

The other cute guys looked on and stroked their cocks. Ben whimpered and shook behind me and his cock pulsed in me. I oozed from my cock into Cathy. She assured me, "Don't worry honey. I can't get pregnant and I know we're both clean." She kissed my cheek.

Another young guy with even faster rabbit thrusts and whimpering quickly replaced Ben. I looked over my shoulder at him. He was so cute with his closed eyes, slightly eye-shadowed, the long mascara laden lashes and eyeliner making them pop. His glossed lips and lightly blushed cheeks combined with it all to make him look like a little angel. His bright eyes opened wide, and he gripped my hips tightly as he let out a girlish squeal and pummeled me like a little boy madly fucking his pillow. I smiled back at him and watched his face as he shoved himself all the way in and held it there while it pulsed inside of me and his face contorted and body shook. I rode the edge of release once more, filled with his passionate energy flowing through me.

Cathy whispered to me, watching him finish fucking me like I was. She beamed. "Isn't he cute? They all are. Each one of them would feminize so well. Like you and Cassie did. You should help them."

He withdrew. I once again realized I was inside of my beautiful doll, Cathy and fucked her tight pussy fervently. My cock was in heaven but I missed having one in my ass.

I humped Cathy making her shudder and shake and pull my ass to her. I was at the edge of coming in her and pounded her as if it would happen any second. She came again under me and rolled her head on her shoulders then grabbed my butt cheeks, digging her nails in and made me stay deep inside and not thrust. "I need a break. Just stay there like that, princess."

I peppered her face with kisses and looked around. Ben was stroking himself watching us and the one that just came in my ass was as well. They were both hard again. The other two were evidently more shy, staying at a distance. They were chubby and cute femboys with plum, round faces with blush on their cheeks and light eye makeup.

I motioned to one of them and he came over. I patted my ass and his eyes lit up as he came around me, slid his cock in my ass and began humping. Motioning the other one to my face, I reached out for his cock to suck. The one in back fucked me nicely while I sucked another luscious cock and tingles and ripples of pleasure ran through me once again at the very oozing edge of a release. Right at the point when it hits the peak and you think it's going to shoot, it doesn't. It was fantastic, but it was also *way* too much stimulation. I'd have to come soon.

I swallowed the come of the cute chubby one fucking my face and the one in my bottom pulsed inside me and squeezed my hips while I continued to ooze into Cathy beneath me while she stroked my hair. I hungered for more and called Ben and the other one back and they obliged me, giving me more sweet femboy cock and their passion. Still, it didn't release me from the monkey on my back. I looked around and all the boys were gone.

Cathy patted my bottom. "Let's take a break okay?"

"Sure." I reluctantly pulled my cock from her and helped her up. We straightened our dresses and adjusted our cleavage then she took my hand and we clicked to the bar and ordered a drink. We sat on the stools and crossed our legs. Cathy held her glass for me to clink. "To a glorious finale for us all."

"That's for sure. I sure could go for the orange pill right now."

She grinned and sipped. She ran her hand on my stockinged thigh sensually. "Still all wound up like a horny girl, huh?"

"Absolutely. Those pills really worked."

"Right." She giggled. "I'm pretty darn satisfied at this point. I'm a little sore from the big black guy too, and from so much fucking in general. I think I'm done."

I whined like a little girl. "Oh Cathy! But I wanted to come in you."

"Maybe next time. Why not come in Cassie. I'm sure she'd love that. Or just jerk off here, looking at me." She giggled. "If that works."

She slid one finger into her crotchless panties, and in her slit while she smiled at me. "I can't wait until we're neighbors." She took my hand, wrapped it around my cock and made me stroke it.

I took her tiny Barbie doll body in and etched her image in my mind. Her firm substantial breasts, shapely legs, tiny feet, narrow waist, bright stellar eyes. She was a vision. She lowered her top, took her breasts out and played with them and the nipples while looking into my eyes. "So, Riley. Do you think you'll stay a girl now that you've experienced all of it?" She licked her lips and sucked her finger.

I jerked myself fervently and nodded. "God yes."

"Do you think you'll get implants? You know, hip, butt, breast, cheek. Would you like that?"

I jerked faster thinking about it. It was thrilling to imagine. "Oh god yes. But I have to save up."

"I bet Josh would take care of that for you girls."

"That would be incredible."

"And did you like those four femboys?"

I nodded, and remembered them making me more intent on coming as my body rode the edge.

"You could help them be girls like you and Cassie. They could probably move in with the three of you."

"Wow. It's hard to imagine all of this happening. It's so incredible. And all we wanted to do was meet a couple of girls and look at all the new friends we have."

"Yup!" She sipped her drink. She looked at my hand stroking my cock. "You know you can come anytime right?"

"I need an orange pill. I need Jill. She has them."

Cathy reached in her purse and took out a clear plastic container with a white lid and a label with orange pills in it. She released one onto her palm and handed it to me. "Now don't swallow it. Just taste it and let it melt." I took it and put it in my mouth hurriedly. She held the container to show me the label.

My eyes opened wide. "Tic Tacs! The others were too!?"

"Uh, huh. The mind is a powerful thing isn't it? You did well tonight and now you deserve to let it all go. Ready?"

I nodded. I could feel it building. I closed my eyes and remembered sucking and being fucked by those femboys. Cathy swiveled my seat to face the others. I sensed their eyes on me. She massaged my shoulders. I leaned my head back while I felt her hand ready to catch my come from the tip. I imagined them coming in me and one gush after another flooded from my cock, my legs twitching and shaking as I whimpered and squeaked.

Cathy whispered. "Good girl, Riley Good girl. Now you can rest and relax." She lifted her palm to me to lick. I lapped it up. She hugged me and took me by the hand.

24

I woke being spooned by an angel. We were upstairs in an empty room in a sleeping bag on the floor, our heads on a pillow. Her arm wrapped over me. I turned in the bag to embrace her and we kissed deeply. I broke the kiss and her eyes popped open and met mine. Her tiny voice greeted me. "Hi Riley!" She stretched her arms and looked toward the window. "It's sunny out and it's just flurrying. I bet we can move you into Josh's today."

"For sure." I looked around for Cassie. She was in a sleeping bag with Ben with her arms cradling him in front of her. "How cute they are."

"They sure are. Do you think she'll want to transform those femboys?"

"I know she will. I know I do. Who could ever pass up giving a gift like this to another femboy. I can't imagine going back to what I was now."

"That's because this is what you always were. You just didn't know it yet."

"I guess. I mean I always loved the feminine. This just makes more sense now." We slid out of the sleeping bag and sat on it. Indian style. "I need my street clothes."

"The bags are downstairs. I can bring them all up when you're ready."

I nodded. "Street clothes."

Cathy ran off and brought them for us. I put on a knee-length corduroy skirt, a thick V-neck sweater, a pair of suede wedge heel boots along with bra and underwear. I stood before Cathy ready to leave. "I love how my clothes fit who I am now."

Cathy slid the back of her tiny hand against my cheek, gazing into my eyes. "I love that too. Who knows? After we get our real jobs and find out where we'll all live and things. Who knows?

Maybe I'll get to keep enjoying my new girlfriend as my wife." She gave me a peck on the lips.

I kissed her back and hugged her. "Yup. Who knows? We'll we have plenty to explore and enjoy in the meantime, right?"

"Right." She dug in her purse and took out a pack of white Tic Tacs and green Tic Tacs. "Want some? They just freshen your breath. Unless of course you want them to do more." She winked. We each took one of each and swallowed them, laughing.

88

If you enjoyed this book, it would be great if you could leave a review and tell a friend about it or blog it out. Thanks!

Barb and Thom

For more of our books, both fiction and non-fiction, in Kindle, paperback and Audible versions, go to:

Amazon:

http://www.amazon.com/Barbara-Deloto/e/B00J21HWA4/

www.ingramcontent.com/pod-product-compliance
Lightning Source LLC
Chambersburg PA
CBHW051801130726